# CLUB TIMES

*For M...*

**When you see a bre...**

I was getting a manicure at the club spa, and when I stepped out for some fresh air I noticed a limo go by. Not a rarity in these parts, but since the window was rolled down, I saw a handsome sheik in the backseat! Well, call me cool as a cucumber, but I spilled coffee all over my new peach skirt. Does anyone know who this sheik is…and if he's single?

This just in: Fiona Carson jetted off to Paris this morning. Did anyone get a chance to submit a souvenir wish list to her? That feisty Carson daughter is going to kick herself for missing the fine male specimen mentioned above. Wouldn't it be a gas if her prim and oh-so-sweet sister Cara Carson charmed this seductive sheik? Hmm… sheik husband or little Eiffel Tower key chain? You choose.

I'd like to take a minute to pay homage to our beloved district attorney Spence Harrison. Basically, we think you're the cat's meow and the wind beneath Mission Creek's wings. Don't blush, Spence. We're rooting for you as you put away the bad guy who killed our judge Carl Bridges. We also hope that someone has the good sense to keep you warm at night.

As always, members, make your best stop of the day right here at the Lone Star Country Club!

## About the Author

### CARLA CASSIDY

doesn't belong to the Lone Star Country Club, but she did marry a prince of a man years ago. Like all the heroines in the Carson family, she was lucky enough to find true love. Carla spends her days writing books and her nights playing love slave to her "prince," which makes them both giggle!

# CARLA CASSIDY

## PROMISED TO A SHEIK

TORONTO  NEW YORK  LONDON
AMSTERDAM  PARIS  SYDNEY  HAMBURG
STOCKHOLM  ATHENS  TOKYO  MILAN  MADRID
PRAGUE  WARSAW  BUDAPEST  AUCKLAND

Special thanks and acknowledgment are given
to Carla Cassidy for her contribution
to the Lone Star Country Club series.

Recycling programs
for this product may
not exist in your area.

ISBN-13: 978-0-373-61356-4

PROMISED TO A SHEIK

Copyright © 2002 by Harlequin Books S.A.

**Printed in U.S.A.**

# Welcome to the

LONE STAR

LS
CC

COUNTRY
CLUB
EST. 1923

*Where Texas society reigns supreme—
and appearances are everything!*

*Seduction and deception course through Mission Creek...*

**Sheik Omar Al Abdar:** This commanding oil tycoon
needs a wife and heirs to continue his bloodline.
He has the perfect woman in mind to fulfill his every
desire. But little does Omar know that the younger
woman who breathlessly pledges "I do" is his intended
bride's smitten twin sister!

**Cara Carson:** She fell head over heels for Sheik Omar
when he courted her sister through his heart-swelling
love letters. It didn't take much to convince her
uninterested sis to let her fill in as Omar's starry-eyed
bride. But would the shy schoolteacher's deception ruin
her one chance at true happiness?

**The Mysterious Waitress:** Waitress "Daisy Parker"
is harboring a shocking secret that could link her to a
high-profile investigation. Will the truth compromise
her perilous mission?

**The Mysterious Mercenary:** MIA millionaire
Luke Callahan is embroiled in a furtive adventure that
could have dire consequences....

# THE FAMILIES

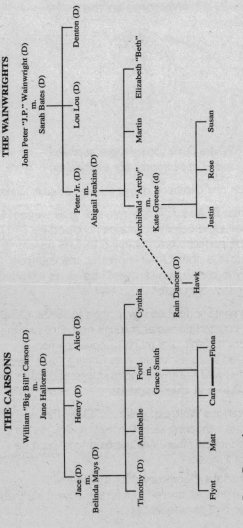

## THE CARSONS

William "Big Bill" Carson (D)
m.
Jane Halloran (D)

- Jace (D)
  m.
  Belinda Mays (D)
- Henry (D)
- Alice (D)

- Timothy (D)
- Annabelle
- Ford
  m.
  Grace Smith
- Cynthia

Flynt — Matt — Cara ▬▬▬ Fiona

## THE WAINWRIGHTS

John Peter "J.P." Wainwright (D)
m.
Sarah Bates (D)

- Peter Jr. (D)
  m.
  Abigail Jenkins (D)
- Lou Lou (D)
- Denton (D)

- Archibald "Archy"
  m.
  Kate Greene (d)
- Martin
- Elizabeth "Beth"

Justin — Rose — Susan

Rain Dancer (D)
|
Hawk

| D | Deceased |
|---|---|
| d | Divorced |
| m. | Married |
| ---- | Affair |
| ▬▬ | Twins |

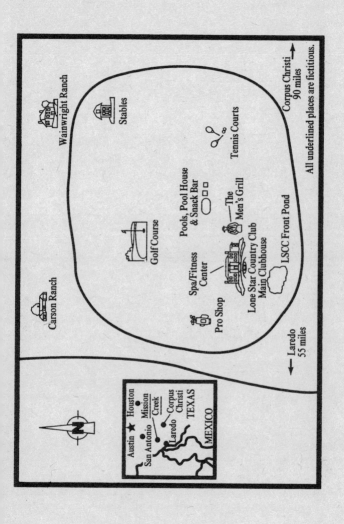

# Chapter 1

"Sheik Al Abdar, could you tell us if this impromptu visit to Texas is for business or pleasure?"

Sheik Omar Al Abdar flashed a slightly cool smile at the female reporter whose voice had risen above the others. He'd only just stepped out of the private jet that had flown him from his small, Middle East country of Gaspar to a private airstrip just outside Mission Creek, Texas.

"I was unaware that the press had been alerted to my presence here in Texas," he replied.

"When one of the most eligible bachelors in the world comes to Texas, Texas sits up and takes notice," the reporter responded with a dazzling smile.

Omar paid her no attention. His mind was focused on his mission.

*What if she says no?* The question came unbidden to Omar's mind and he shoved it away, refusing to consider the possibility.

Rashad Aziz held up his hands to halt the volley of questions. "Please, please, His Royal Highness has traveled a long distance today and is eager to get to his destination. He will answer no questions at this time."

As if on an unspoken cue, several guards moved into position, shielding Sheik Omar from the small crowd of reporters as they ushered him toward an awaiting car.

"Thank you, Rashad." Omar smiled at his personal assistant once they were all settled in the car and pulling away from the circle of reporters. "It would appear the owner of the airstrip leaked the information about our arrival here."

Rashad Aziz, a petite man in his fifties with skin the color of a coconut shell and a cynicism Omar often found amusing, grimaced. "I'm sure he was paid handsomely for giving the information to those vultures."

Rashad withdrew a small pad from his breast pocket. "We have made arrangements for you at the Brighton Hotel in Mission Creek. The Ashbury Suite will be yours for as long as you like. I spoke to the owner of the hotel myself, and he has assured me that his entire staff is eager to see that your every wish is granted."

"I'm sure it will be just fine," Omar said absently.

"And now you will tell the driver that we will go to the Carson Ranch before checking into the hotel."

Rashad didn't blink an eye even though the plan had been for Omar to go immediately to his hotel. Rashad moved to the seat directly behind the limo driver and quickly relayed the change in plans. He remained seated there, as if instinctively recognizing that the sheik wanted a few moments with his own thoughts.

Omar stared out the window at the passing landscape. It irritated him that the press knew he was here. He'd hoped to fly into Mission Creek, accomplish his goal, then return to Gaspar without the glare of the media upon him.

He did not want the press to be privy to his personal business, and this trip to Texas was strictly personal. When he succeeded, he'd be more than happy for the world to know what he'd done.

*What if she says no?* Again the question came from nowhere to plague him with the disturbing possibility. He reached into his breast pocket and withdrew a photograph.

The picture was of a young woman in a shimmering silver ball gown. The dark brown wavy hair that framed her heart-shaped face complemented her peaches-and-cream complexion. He remembered her eyes had been like emeralds, flirting and dancing and surrounded by thick, long lashes. A beauty mark at the corner of her mouth drew attention to the lush, thoroughly kissable-looking lips.

Elizabeth Fiona Carson. She'd been twenty-one years old when the photo was taken at a cotillion Omar had attended in this very town. That had been six years ago—and now he had come to claim her as his bride.

*What if she says no?*

He tucked the photo back in his pocket and straightened up in the seat. Of course she would not say no. He was Sheik Omar Al Abdar, King of Gaspar. Any woman would be proud to be chosen by him as his wife.

As the driver turned onto the Carson property, Omar once again turned his attention out the window. The Carson ranch was known throughout Texas for the quality of its cattle, but he was more interested in the fact that this was Elizabeth's home, the place of her birth and her upbringing.

In the letters they had exchanged over the past year, she had spoken of this place and of her parents with great affection.

Although not nearly as big as his palace back in Gaspar, the main house was certainly impressive. A large porch ran the length of the front of the massive house, along with dozens of large windows.

The grounds were well kept, manicured to perfection and with aesthetically pleasing flower gardens and an abundance of trees.

As the car began to turn into the half-moon driveway in front of the house, Omar leaned forward. "No," he said. "Not the main house. There should be a caretaker's cottage somewhere on the premises." He pointed to an offshoot drive that led past a four-car garage. "There. Go there."

The driver did his bidding, passing the garage and other outbuildings. In the distance Omar spied the small cottage where he knew Elizabeth lived.

He knew it not only from the letters she'd written him, but by the baskets of flowers that hung from the small porch. She'd told him she loved flowers.

As the car came to a halt before the little cottage, Omar felt a curious fluttering in the pit of his stomach. It couldn't be nerves, he thought. He was a sheik, the king of his country. He didn't get nervous, he made other people nervous.

Hunger. Surely that was what made his stomach roll. They had traveled all day to arrive in Texas, and their last meal had been far too long ago.

Rashad opened the door to allow him to step out. With a head full of thoughts about the woman inside the cottage, Omar absently smoothed a hand down the front of his Armani suit, hoping he didn't appear too travel-rumpled.

As Omar walked up to the front door, his two body-guards stationed themselves on either side of the porch and Rashad returned to the back of the limo.

Omar drew a deep breath, aware that this would be one of the defining moments of his life. At thirty-eight years old, it was far past time he claimed a bride, and even though he hadn't seen Elizabeth Fiona Carson for six years, she was the woman he had chosen to make his wife.

He knocked on the door, at the same time aware of the sweet scent of the nearby flower baskets. He made a mental note to ensure there were always fresh-cut flowers in her rooms at the palace.

The door opened, and Omar gazed at his bride-to-be. "Elizabeth," he said. In an instant he drank in the sight of her, pleased that she looked just as he remembered.

"Omar!" Her brilliant green eyes widened in shock at the same time her hands raced first to her hair, then to smooth down the front of her dress.

Even though her dark wavy hair was slightly tousled and the denim dress she wore was rather plain, she looked lovely, and the desire he'd felt for her on that night so long ago sprang to life as if the six intervening years had never occurred.

"Wha—what are you doing here? I didn't know you were coming to Texas. I just got your last letter today, and you didn't mention a word about coming here." She bit her bottom lip, as if aware she was rambling.

Omar found the rambling charming. He smiled at her, more certain than ever of what he was about to do. "I didn't let you know I was coming to Texas because I wanted to surprise you."

"You've certainly done that," she replied. "Uh, would you like to come in?"

"I would not be so thoughtless as to appear unannounced on your doorstep and expect you to entertain me," he replied. "I have yet to check in to my hotel, but I wanted to stop here first and ask you an important question."

"Question?" She still looked stunned by his appearance. Again she raked a hand through her hair, and he noticed her hand trembled slightly. "What kind of a question?"

He captured her fluttering hand in his, and again her beautiful green eyes widened. He could smell her fragrance, a floral scent that instantly reminded him of the night at the cotillion.

She had bewitched him that night, blatantly flirting and charming every man in attendance, and Omar had been no exception. But at that time Omar had been no more ready for marriage than she had been.

"Elizabeth, I've come to tell you how much I have enjoyed our correspondence over the past year, that through your letters I feel as if I have come to know your mind and your heart."

Her eyes seemed to grow even wider, and he tightened his hand around hers. "Elizabeth Fiona Carson, I have come to Texas to claim you as my wife. Will you marry me?"

Elizabeth Cara Carson stared at the handsome man before her, fighting against the panic that urged her to jerk her hand away, turn and flee into the cottage.

*This can't be happening,* she thought frantically. "Omar...I...I...this is so sudden," she finally managed to say as she pulled her hand from his. In truth, this was not only sudden, it was a disaster!

"I have taken you by surprise," he said, stating the obvious.

"That's certainly an understatement." She had known from the photos she'd seen of him since their one and only meeting six years ago that he had matured into a devastatingly handsome man.

However, no picture had prepared her for the dark, liquid warmth of his eyes, or the impossible width of his broad shoulders. No pictures had prepared her for the hard, masculine planes of his face, a masculinity tempered by long, dark eyelashes and a soft smile.

Omar nodded. "I will leave you now to contemplate my proposal. Would you do me the honor of having lunch with me tomorrow? We can discuss our future at that time. I'm staying at the Brighton downtown."

"Lunch?" she echoed.

"I will send a car for you at noon. Does that sound all right?" His dark eyes were bottomless pools that beckoned her in. But she averted her gaze from his, refusing to fall into the seductive depths.

She was in trouble—big trouble—and perhaps by noon the next day she would be able to get it all sorted out.

"That would be fine," she agreed. "Lunch tomorrow. I'll be ready at noon."

"Good. I look forward to it." He gave her a small, formal bow, then turned on his heels and headed back to his awaiting car.

*Our future.* The words rang in Cara's ears as she watched the stretch limo disappear from her sight. The minute the car was gone, she flew into the cottage and grabbed the phone.

Fiona. She had to get in touch with Fiona. Quickly she punched in the numbers that would ring in her sister's quarters at the main house.

*"You know I want to talk to you."* Fiona's voice purred in Cara's ear. *"Unfortunately, I'm not here at the moment, but please leave your name—"*

Cara hung up, suddenly remembering that that morning her sister had been whining over the fact it was Saturday night and she didn't have a date. Fiona had decided to spend the unusual free Saturday night at Body Perfect, the spa in the Lone Star Country Club.

Cara grabbed her car keys and left her cottage. She had to talk to Fiona. She had to tell her that Sheik Omar was here, in Texas, and had just proposed marriage to her—only, he thought *she* was Fiona. Things were suddenly a major mess.

It took only minutes for Cara to reach the Lone Star Country Club. As always as she pulled up in front of the impressive four-story pink granite building, a swell of pride filled her heart.

The resort and country club was part of her legacy, built partially on Carson land by her grandfather and a neighbor, J. P. Wainwright, in 1923. In the intervening years the country club had become world renowned for its luxury, many amenities and top-notch staff.

But Cara's pride lasted only a moment, quickly swallowed by the imminent need to talk to her sister.

She parked her car beneath the covered portico and jumped out. "Hi, Larry," she said to the awaiting valet.

"Ms. Carson, nice to see you again," he said as he took her keys from her.

"I shouldn't be too long," she said, then flew through the doors that led to the huge lobby. She nodded and smiled to the people she knew as she hurried to the elevators.

Body Perfect, the ladies' spa and beauty salon was located on the second floor. The receptionist greeted her in surprise. "Cara!" She frowned and looked at her computer screen. "I didn't realize you had an appointment this evening."

"I don't. I just need to speak to my sister," Cara replied. "Can you tell me where she is?"

"She has an appointment for a massage with Heidi in fifteen minutes, and I think she was going into the sauna before her massage."

"Thanks," Cara said, then rushed toward the changing room just outside the sauna.

As she changed her clothes and grabbed one of the white, fluffy body towels provided, she thought of that moment when she'd opened her door and seen Sheik Omar on her front porch.

She wouldn't have been more stunned if the Easter bunny had been standing there in all his floppy-eared splendor.

Omar had asked for her hand in marriage. Cara's

stomach clenched. Suddenly the harmless little deceit she and Fiona had indulged in for the past year didn't seem so harmless anymore.

Fiona would know what to do. Fiona was good at extricating herself from trouble. Cara opened the door and stepped into the steamy mists of the sauna.

She instantly spied her sister, prone on one of the benches, a hand towel covering her face. She was thankful there was nobody else using the facility at the moment.

"Fiona," Cara said as she poked her sister in the side.

Fiona yelped and grabbed the towel from her face. "Cara, what are you doing here?" she asked in surprise. She sat up and faced Cara.

The two women were identical twins. The only difference was the location of their beauty marks. Cara's was just above her lips on the left side and Fiona's was just above her lips on the right side. Mirror images.

"We're in trouble," Cara said without preamble. She sat down next to her sister on the bench. "Guess who showed up on my front doorstep ten minutes ago?"

"I can't imagine." Fiona raked her fingers through her damp hair.

"Sheik Omar Al Abdar." Cara watched as her twin sister's green eyes widened in shock. "He asked me to marry him, Fiona."

Fiona stared at her another moment, then threw back her head and laughed. "Oh, this is just too amusing!"

Cara swallowed a sigh of irritation. Fiona never took anything seriously. "Fiona, the man proposed to me, but he thinks I'm you."

Fiona eyed her sister curiously. "What on earth did you write in those letters to inspire a marriage proposal?"

Cara shrugged. "Just stuff," she replied. Her dreams, her hopes, her innermost thoughts—that was what she had written to Sheik Omar, and at the end of each letter she had signed her sister's name.

Fiona waved a hand dismissively. "Well, I'm certainly not going to marry any sheik," she exclaimed. "Besides, if I remember correctly, Sheik Omar is old."

"He isn't old," Cara instantly protested, thinking of the man she'd seen only minutes earlier. "He's only thirty-eight." And he'd looked as fit and as virile as any twenty-year-old, she mentally added. "He's quite handsome and he wants to have lunch tomorrow to discuss our future together."

"So, have lunch with him and keep your mouth shut." Even through the steam, Cara could see the bright sparkle of her sister's eyes. "Oh, Cara, have a little fun with this!"

"I couldn't do that," Cara said softly, although Fiona's words held a provocative appeal. "He should know the truth."

"Why? Why does he need to know that I got tired of writing him letters and you kept up the correspondence with him?"

She grabbed Cara's hands in hers. "Your life is such

a bore. I'm not saying you have to actually marry him, but you're twenty-seven years old and have never had anything exciting happen in your life—other than that dreadful incident last year in school. Wouldn't you love to have a great story to tell your grandchildren someday?"

The "dreadful incident" was what had prompted Cara to decide not to renew her contract as an English teacher at the high school for this year.

"The way my love life is going, I'll probably never have grandchildren," she replied softly.

"Of course you will," Fiona exclaimed. "You're the type who will eventually fall madly in love and settle for a life of simple domesticity, complete with kids and a dog."

Cara grinned. "You make it sound like a fate worse than death."

"It's fine for other women." Fiona grinned impudently. "I just have loftier ideas for myself." Her grin faded and once again she reached for Cara's hands. "Go for it, Cara. How many times in your life are you going to be able to be engaged to a sheik?"

Cara said nothing, for a moment remembering the warmth of Omar's hand around hers, the sweet appeal in the depths of his eyes. Would it be so terrible to pretend for just a couple of days to be Elizabeth Fiona Carson instead of Elizabeth Cara Carson?

Certainly she would love to get an opportunity to talk in person to the man whose letters had so touched her heart. She would love to spend just a little bit of time being somebody special in his life.

"Go for it. I'll even make it easier on you," Fiona said, pulling Cara from her inward thoughts.

"What do you mean?"

Fiona took the hand towel and dabbed at her forehead. "I've been so utterly bored the past couple of weeks that I've been toying with the idea of taking a little vacation. First thing in the morning I'll hop a jet to Paris for a week or two. That way I'll be out of town and there will be no chance that Omar will realize you aren't me."

Cara was silent for a moment, thinking of all the reasons she shouldn't indulge in such a subterfuge, yet unable to still the sweet anticipation that rushed through her as she realized she was going to do it.

"And, Cara, if you are going to be me, please do me justice," Fiona said dryly. Then she placed the towel over her face and once again stretched out on the bench.

*Just for a couple of days,* Cara told herself minutes later as she showered, then dressed once again. She would pretend to be the woman Omar had been so taken with at the cotillion, the woman whose signature she'd signed to the dozens of letters she'd written him.

Just for a couple of days she wanted the opportunity to shine in somebody else's eyes. In Omar's eyes. Eventually she would tell him she couldn't marry him, and he would return to Gaspar none the wiser.

It seemed a foolproof plan, but Cara had a feeling the only fool in the whole plan might just be her, for even contemplating such an adventure.

As Cara Carson left the Lone Star Country Club, two waitresses in the country club's Yellow Rose Café went on break together.

"So, Daisy, do you have any big plans for the rest of the weekend?" Ginger Walton asked, as the two sat down at the small table in the break room.

Haley Mercado, who for the past six months had been pretending to be Daisy Parker, smiled at Ginger. The auburn-haired, blue-eyed young woman had, in the past couple of months, become a good friend. "Yeah, I'm working tonight, then I'm working tomorrow night."

Ginger laughed. "Me, too. At least working all these hours keeps us out of trouble, right?"

"Right," Haley replied, although nothing could be further from the truth in her case. She was in a world of trouble.

Working undercover for the FBI, Haley was not only pretending to be somebody she wasn't, she was also tied emotionally and by blood to one of the most powerful families in the Texas Mafia. And that was just the beginning of her woes.

"Just think," Ginger continued as she opened a bag of potato chips. "Maybe someday we'll be here waiting tables with tired feet and sore backs and our

Prince Charmings will waltz in and take us away from all this."

Haley snorted in appropriate Daisy-like fashion. "Honey, I gave up on the notion of Prince Charming a long time ago," she exclaimed in the thick accent she'd adopted for her new persona.

"Not me," Ginger replied, a dreamy expression in her eyes. "I'm not looking for a man to take care of me or anything like that," she hurriedly added. "I've been taking care of myself for a long time. But it would be nice to have somebody special to share my life with, somebody who adored me as much as I adored him."

Ginger's words stirred a memory in Haley, one she rarely allowed to surface in her mind. A single night of passion spent in the arms of the man she'd loved from afar for years. Her heart ached as she thought of the consequence of that night.

She shoved away the memory, knowing that to indulge herself in thoughts of the past and that man would only make her life now more difficult. And things were difficult enough already.

"Where does Harvey have you stationed for tomorrow night?" Ginger asked.

"The Men's Grill," Haley replied.

"Lucky you, the tips are always good in there," Ginger replied.

*Yeah, lucky me,* Haley thought. She'd already told her contacts at the FBI that she was assigned to the grill the following night. That meant when she came to work the next evening she'd be wired, and her goal would be to record any conversations that might take place that could bring down the Mafia.

The temporary Men's Grill was the place where power was wielded, deals were made, and bargains were sealed. In the smoky confines of the private bar and restaurant, "the family" met to conduct business.

"The family" included members of her family, the Mercados, and part of her deal with the FBI was that she would help tumble the Mafia in exchange for immunity for her father, Johnny, and her brother, Ricky.

However, there was one man Haley hoped to bring to his knees. Frank Del Brio. His very name caused a chill of fear to race up her spine. Fear coupled with rage.

Since the death of Carmine Mercado, the head of the "family," there had been rumors that her brother was the logical choice to take his place. Haley had also heard rumors that Frank Del Brio was acting as if he was already the new don.

But that wasn't why Haley wanted to see him arrested and locked up for the rest of his life.

Frank Del Brio had briefly been her fiancé. It had been because of him that she'd had to fake her own death and was now working with the FBI. He'd been responsible for her estrangement from her family, for the plastic surgery she'd undergone to transform her features and for the murder of her mother.

"Hey, am I paying you two to sit in here all night?" Harvey Small, the manager of the Lone Star Country

Club, stuck his head into the break room. "Break is over. I need you on the floor."

"Back to the salt mines," Ginger said. She crumpled up her empty chip bag, tossed it into the nearby trash container, then stood.

"Yeah, no rest for the wicked," Haley said, also standing.

Maybe tomorrow night she would get the information the FBI needed and the mob would be busted. Frank would be thrown in jail, and Haley could reclaim her life. She could be reunited with all the people she loved.

And maybe tomorrow night Frank Del Brio would recognize her beneath her disguise and all would be lost. She shoved this frightening thought out of her head as she and Ginger hurried back to work.

## *Chapter 2*

She dreamed of him all night long. She dreamed of Sheik Omar Al Abdar and a beautiful foreign land called Gaspar, which he had described in one of his letters as a gemstone afloat on the sea.

In those dreams of Omar, he had gazed at her with his beautiful eyes and told her that he loved her more than anyone else on earth, and he called her Cara instead of Fiona. She'd awakened with a fierce longing, wishing that her dream would become a reality.

It was just before noon when Cara stood before her bathroom mirror, checking her reflection to make sure she looked all right for lunch with a sheik.

The dreams had stirred a wistfulness inside her, a longing to see the country that Omar had written about so eloquently in his letters, a longing to spend

time with the man who had written such beautiful
words.

The woman in the mirror who stared back at her
wore a small frown. She had searched through her
closet, trying to find something to wear that might be
something Fiona would choose. But Fiona and Cara
had completely different taste in clothing.

Fiona was like a brilliant flower, partial to vivid
colors and cutting-edge styles. Cara was far more conservative, bland and boring. Her frown deepened, and
she consciously smoothed it away and smiled at her
reflection.

She'd found the jade-colored dress in the back of
her closet with the tags still attached. She'd bought it
on a whim, although it wasn't her usual conventional
style. The scoop neckline was a little risqué for her
and the flirty skirt was definitely shorter than what
she normally wore. The dress was more the type that
Fiona would wear, which was why she had chosen to
wear it today.

A wave of guilt swept through her and she turned
away from the mirror. She was consciously planning
on impersonating her sister for the first time in years.

As children they had occasionally fooled people
by pretending to be each other. Those were childish
games with no real consequences. But she and Fiona
weren't children anymore, and her impersonation of
Fiona had prompted an important man to travel thou-
sands of miles to propose.

Just for a couple of days, she told herself. Surely

there was no harm in continuing the pretense for a couple of days. What memories these days would provide her in the future!

Her heart leaped up to her throat as a knock fell on her door. A quick glance at her watch told her it was time for Omar to pick her up.

She just hoped she could pull this off. She grabbed her purse from the sofa and she was surprised to open the door and see not Omar, but rather a short, thin man.

"Good afternoon, Ms. Carson. My name is Rashad Aziz. I am the personal assistant for Sheik Al Abdar. He is awaiting your company for lunch."

Cara smoothed a hand down the skirt of her dress and nodded. "I'm ready to go," she replied.

The little man smiled in delight. "Ah, a rare woman—one who is ready on time." He escorted her to the waiting limo. When she was safely ensconced in the back, he shut the door, then took a position in the passenger seat next to the driver.

She wished Rashad had joined her in the back of the limo. Perhaps he might have chatted with her and she wouldn't be thinking about what a huge mistake all this was.

As the limo pulled out of the Carson property and headed toward town, Cara told herself again that everything would be all right. She was certain the sheik wouldn't remain in town long, that he would need to return to his country fairly quickly.

In the meantime she could enjoy a couple of dates

with him, then turn down his marriage proposal. He would entertain fond memories of Fiona, and Cara would have wonderful memories of being dated by a handsome sheik who had shown in his letters his gentle, kind nature.

Dating had always been difficult for her. Although Mission Creek had more than its share of handsome, eligible bachelors, most of them at one time or another had dated Fiona. And Cara had made it a personal decision never to date a man who had dated her twin sister.

Cara never wanted to worry about being a second choice, a pale imitation of what the man wanted but couldn't have. She never wanted to wonder if the man was dating her because she was a replica of her sister.

However, Fiona's fickle dating style made it difficult for Cara to *find* men her sister hadn't dated.

Omar hadn't dated Fiona. He knew Fiona only through her letters. Letters Cara had written. Granted, he'd spent several hours with Fiona at a cotillion six years before, but it hadn't been a date.

That night Fiona had played the role of belle of the ball, flitting from man to man in true Scarlett O'Hara fashion. Cara had, as usual, blended into the woodwork, watching the festivities rather than participating in them.

She had been introduced to Omar that night, but knew he probably didn't remember her at all. Her gown had been a pale pink and she hadn't tried to compete with her sister for male attention.

She'd watched him that night—watched him watching Fiona—and she'd thought him one of the most handsome men she'd ever seen.

Her heart beat faster as the limo entered the small town of Mission Creek. Ahead she could see the Brighton Hotel, and knew the eight-story luxury building was where they were going. Not only was it exorbitantly expensive with a five-star rating, but also it was the only hotel in the small town of Mission Creek aside from the accommodations at the Lone Star Country Club.

As the limo pulled to a halt before the gold-trimmed glass front doors, a uniformed valet stepped forward. Rashad jumped out of the car and waved the valet away.

He opened the door for her, his smile exposing perfect white teeth. "I will escort you to where Sheik Al Abdar awaits."

He led her through the front doors and into the posh lobby. The furnishings were in burgundy and gold, with lush green plants providing the accenting green.

Cara had spent little time in the hotel before, and looked around with interest. When her family planned dinners or gatherings, they always took place at the Lone Star Country Club.

When they reached the back end of the lobby, Rashad led her through a doorway that entered into the Gold Room Restaurant.

There were several people seated at the tables, but Omar wasn't one of the diners in the dimly lit room.

It wasn't until they reached another door at the back of the restaurant that Cara realized Omar must have reserved a private dining room.

Two men stood on either side of the door. Judging by the thickness of their necks and their stern demeanor, Cara guessed they were bodyguards to the sheik.

Rashad gestured toward the door and smiled once again. "Sheik Al Abdar awaits you," he said.

She'd thought dining with the sheik would be relatively safe. After all, it would be difficult to have too private a conversation with other diners talking, with the clink of silver and glassware all around them.

As she eyed the door before her, trepidation swept through her. A private dining room meant...well, privacy. She would have to be on her toes to make him believe she was the same woman he'd seen the night of the cotillion.

Drawing a deep breath, she knocked.

Omar opened the door, his handsome face lit with a smile that instantly warmed her. "Elizabeth," he said as he took her hand in his and pulled her across the threshold. "You look positively stunning." He closed the door behind them.

"Thank you," she murmured, then exclaimed in surprise as she looked around the small room. Fresh-cut flowers were everywhere, bouquets of them that filled the room with their sweet fragrance.

She stepped over to an arrangement of multicolored roses on top of a marble stand, and drew a deep breath. "Oh, Omar, they are all so lovely."

He smiled. "I remembered you love flowers. I hope they please you."

"Please me? How could I not be pleased?" She was touched beyond belief. First because he remembered she'd mentioned in one of her letters how much she liked flowers, and second because he had gone out of his way to fill the room with them for her.

"Please have a seat." He gestured toward the small table in the middle of the room. In the center of the table two candles were lit, their warm glow flickering on the crystal glasses and gold tableware.

Cara sat in one of the chairs, then gasped in surprise as he turned off the overhead light, plunging the windowless room into candlelight intimacy.

She became conscious of soft music playing in the background and realized the scene was set for romance. Her heart pounded as her nervousness increased.

As Omar took the seat opposite her, a waiter appeared through a doorway she hadn't noticed in the back of the room. He held a bottle of wine and wore a deferential smile.

"I took the liberty of ordering the wine," Omar said. "I hope you don't mind."

"Not at all," she assured him, as the waiter filled their glasses. When the waiter was finished, he disappeared once again.

Omar picked up his wineglass and held it out toward her. "To the future. May it bring us much happiness."

It was a toast Cara could make without a twinge of conscience. After all, he hadn't said "to us," which would have been difficult for her to toast to since she knew there wouldn't be an "us."

Omar took a sip of his wine, then leaned back in his chair, a look of intense satisfaction on his face as his gaze lingered on her. "You are as beautiful as I remember," he said, his voice a deep verbal caress. "Actually, the past six years have only made you more beautiful."

Cara felt color sweep up into her cheeks. "And you are as handsome as I remember," she replied.

Today he was once again dressed in Western wear. His black suit fit him to perfection, and the white shirt was monogrammed at the sleeves with his initials. But it wasn't his clothes that threatened to steal her breath away.

Beneath the suit jacket, his shoulders looked broad and strong. The slacks displayed the long length of his legs, and the white shirt emphasized the attractive olive coloring of his skin.

Beneath his dark, thick eyebrows, his ebony eyes caressed her as he smiled at her compliment, flashing his beautiful white teeth. "We will make a very attractive married couple."

He seemed to recognize she was about to protest

and held up his hand to still her. "But we will talk of other things first."

Cara relaxed slightly. She didn't want to think about the marriage proposal he'd offered the day before. She just wanted to enjoy being here with him now. "Your trip to the States was pleasant, I hope," she said, wanting to find a safe topic.

"Very pleasant," he replied, and took another sip of his wine. She noticed the ring on his hand, an opulent emerald surrounded by diamonds. It was a large ring, but didn't in any way dwarf his hands.

She wondered what those big hands would feel like slowly caressing the length of her body. She quickly took another sip of her wine to dispel the heat the thought evoked in her.

"So, tell me, Elizabeth, you are enjoying your time away from the classroom?"

"Yes and no," she replied. She set down her glass and straightened her napkin in her lap. "I've been enjoying my free time, but I have to admit that too much free time is boring."

"I was very surprised to discover that you were a teacher. When I met you years ago at the cotillion, I never would have guessed that would become your profession. At that time you seemed far too adventurous to choose such a conservative job."

"That was six years ago, Omar. Six years is a long time. People change. I've changed." Maybe she could convince him that Fiona had grown more serious, less colorful over the years.

"Yes, and I've seen the changes in you through your letters. Initially they were quite frivolous and entertaining, and I enjoyed them tremendously. But, as our correspondence continued, I saw you maturing—and I still enjoyed your letters."

The change he had seen in the letters was the point where Fiona had tired of writing him and Cara had taken over.

He smiled again and leaned forward, and in the depths of his eyes she saw the flames of simmering emotion. "I know that beneath your maturity and sensitivity is also the woman who is exciting and adventurous. You have become a perfect blend of an audacious enchantress and an insightful, thoughtful woman."

*An audacious enchantress?*

Maybe in her next lifetime, but certainly not in this one. "Omar," she began, realizing she had to tell him the truth.

But, before any more words could leave her lips, the waiter once again appeared at their table with menus. *After dinner I'll tell him,* she thought as she accepted the oversize menu.

After dinner she'd tell him the truth—that she wasn't the enchanting, audacious Fiona who had matured, but rather just plain old boring Cara.

Omar had never felt as right about anything as he did about making her his wife. Every moment that ticked by in her company reassured him that his decision to marry her was good.

Although there would be some in his country who would be irked that he'd chosen an American as his bride, for the most part he knew his subjects would rejoice in the fact that he had finally married and would begin to work on producing heirs. She would win over any of the critics with her beauty, warmth and charm.

When they had placed their orders and the waiter had departed, Omar once again focused his attention on Elizabeth. She had only grown more lovely over the years.

The jade of her dress made her eyes appear an impossible green, and each time she leaned forward he was gifted with a teasing glimpse of the thrust of her breasts. He'd also noticed before she took her seat that her short skirt had displayed legs that were long and slender.

This was a woman who had enough class to be an asset to him in his role as sheik. And this was a woman who was pretty enough, sexy enough, to be an asset to him as a man.

"Your parents are well?" he asked.

"They're fine." She picked up her wineglass once again and took another sip.

"And your sister?"

"She's okay. She's visiting friends in Paris."

He noticed her hand trembled slightly as she set her wineglass back on the table.

She was nervous. The realization surprised him.

And yet, when he thought about it he shouldn't be surprised. Although they had corresponded frequently, had shared intimate thoughts and dreams in letters, a paper relationship was far different from a personal one.

In truth, he was a bit nervous himself. He had made up his mind that she was the woman for him; he was tired of the bachelor game and was ready to be a one-woman man. But he wasn't certain she would accept his marriage proposal. The thought that she might not was simply unacceptable.

Still, he knew the worst thing he could do was rush her. Women were such funny creatures, so driven by emotion. Despite his impatience to see this matter taken care of, he knew he needed to proceed slowly.

"I was surprised to see so many changes here in Mission Creek since my last visit," he said.

She laughed, and his breath caught in his throat at the musical sound. "The locals are always moaning about the fact that nothing much changes in Mission Creek."

"Perhaps the changes here have been so slow in coming that people haven't noticed them, unlike the changes taking place in Gaspar."

She tilted her head, her eyes filled with curiosity. "What's been happening in Gaspar?"

"We have become an extremely wealthy country with the discovery of so many oil fields. And with wealth comes progress."

"But isn't progress good?"

How the candlelight loved her features, he thought. The warm glow fired her emerald eyes with brilliance, complemented her smooth, creamy complexion and emphasized the enchanting beauty mark near her lush lips.

Her beauty had captivated him the night they had first met. He would have staked his claim on her then, but at twenty-one she'd been too young to take on the responsibilities that came with being his wife. And in truth, at that time he'd not been ready to settle down to his own responsibilities.

"Omar?"

He started, realizing he'd been staring at her and hadn't answered her question. "Certainly progress can be a good thing, as long as it is balanced with some of the old traditions and values of the country. There have been some tensions between the people in Gaspar—the ones who want to cling solely to the old ways and the ones who are eager to embrace everything new. In the months and years ahead I hope to herald in a new era—a healthy combination of both."

"In one of your letters, you mentioned that it was your hope that no child of Gaspar would ever go to sleep hungry."

He was touched that she remembered what he had written to her in one of his early letters. "Yes, the social services programs are coming along very well. Most of the people of Gaspar are prospering, but I guess there are always poor people in every country."

The arrival of their dinner interrupted anything

more he was going to say. For the next few minutes they spoke of their favorite foods and the different cities where they had enjoyed good meals.

That led naturally into a discussion of the places they had visited around the world, although Omar confessed that he didn't particularly care to travel but preferred remaining in Gaspar.

"In fact, this trip will have to be relatively brief, as I am in negotiations with several countries concerning the sale of our oil," he said, once their plates had been taken away and they were lingering over coffee. "But enough about all that. I want to hear about you."

"I'm afraid if all we talk about is my life, you'll find the conversation dreadfully dull," she said.

He found her self-deprecation enchanting. A woman as vital, as bold as he remembered her to be could never be boring. "On the contrary," he said. "I find everything about you utterly fascinating."

The blush that covered her cheeks both surprised and delighted him.

"And I find you almost overwhelmingly charming," she murmured.

He laughed, then leaned forward, his gaze holding hers intently. "Good. I want to overwhelm you, romance you and seduce you into agreeing to be my wife."

A tiny frown crossed her brow. "Surely there are lots of women in Gaspar who would desire to marry you," she replied.

He nodded and grinned. "Hundreds." His grin

faded and he replied more seriously, "But none of them has managed to capture my heart the way you have done."

Her green eyes danced teasingly. "You've been described as a tough but wise ruler, and a ruthless, fickle ladies' man."

"Ah, you've been reading the press. Don't you know you aren't supposed to believe everything you read?" He reached across the table and took one of her hands in his.

She had small, dainty hands with fingernails painted a delicate pink. Her fingers were cool, but warmed quickly with the contact.

"Elizabeth, I confess that I have been something of a ladies' man in the past. I was seeking the perfect woman—a woman intelligent enough to sit at my side and help me achieve my goals for my country, a woman sensitive enough to tune in to the needs of my people. And a woman passionate enough to match my own passionate nature. I believe I have found that woman in you."

"Omar, you can't know that for sure. We hardly know each other," she protested. She attempted to pull her hand back, but he held fast.

"I know of your intelligence and sensitivity through the letters we have exchanged. And I know of your passionate nature simply by looking into your eyes." With his free hand he fumbled in his breast pocket and withdrew the ring case that had been resting there.

Her eyes widened at the sight of it, but she said nothing.

"Elizabeth, you captured my fancy six years ago when I first met you, and you've never been far from my mind. In the past year of our correspondence, I've only grown more certain that you are the woman I want for my wife."

He released her hand to open the ring box. She gasped as the ring was exposed. It was a replica of his own ring, only smaller. A large flawless emerald with brilliant diamonds sparkling around the perimeter.

"I had this made especially for you after much thought about what kind of gemstone was right for you. I chose the emerald because it reminds me of how your eyes sparkled and danced on the night of the cotillion so long ago."

"It's stunning," she said softly.

He took her hand in his once again. "No, it will only really be stunning when you're wearing it." He slid the ring onto her finger, pleased that it seemed to be a perfect fit.

"Omar...I'm really not sure—"

He held up a hand to still her. He didn't want to hear what she was about to say. "Please, Elizabeth, wear the ring. Don't deny me the pleasure of seeing it on your hand. We can discuss our future in the days to come. But for now, wear the ring."

He could see her hesitation. She frowned and looked down at the ring for a moment. Finally she gazed at him. "All right," she said. "I'll wear it for now, but I'm not making any promises. I need some time. This has all been an enormous surprise."

At that moment Rashad entered the dining room. "I am sorry to disturb you," he said apologetically. He turned to address Omar. "There is a phone call for you. It concerns the negotiations with Cyprus."

Omar frowned, knowing the oil negotiations were too important to dismiss. As Rashad left the room, Omar stood. "I fear I must take this call, and I don't know how long it might last. Please feel free to finish your coffee or order dessert. Then the car will take you back home."

"No, I'm ready to leave, as well," she said. She dabbed her mouth with her napkin, then stood, and together they walked to the door.

He started to open the door, then changed his mind and turned back to her. "There's just one thing before you go," he said.

"What?"

He gave her no opportunity to anticipate him. In one swift moment he gathered her into his arms and claimed her lips with his.

She stiffened briefly, then relaxed against him, giving herself to his kiss in a response that electrified him.

The kiss lasted only a few seconds, but it was enough for him to taste the heat of her sweet lips and the passion that he'd sensed resided inside her. It was enough for him to know that he wanted this woman more than he'd wanted a woman in a very long time.

When he released her, she looked slightly dazed, and he ran a thumb down her smooth cheek. "I want you as my wife, Elizabeth, and I am a man accustomed to getting what I want. And now Rashad will see you home."

Without waiting for her reply, he opened the door and strode out.

# Chapter 3

"Tell me all about it," Fiona demanded.

It was just after nine, and Cara had been sitting at her kitchen table having a cup of tea when the phone rang for the second time that morning.

"Tell you about what?" she asked teasingly.

"You know what I'm talking about," Fiona exclaimed. Her impatience was obvious, all the way from Paris. "Arabian nights...magic carpets. What I really want to know is if you rubbed Aladdin's lamp?"

"Elizabeth Fiona!" Cara exclaimed, then smiled as she heard her sister's wicked giggle. "And the answer to your ridiculous question is no."

"Ah, too bad. But, seriously, did you have a good time with him?"

Cara looked down at the ring on her finger, noting

how the morning sunshine streaking through her windows played on the diamonds and made the emerald shine as if filled with brilliant green Christmas lights. "I had a wonderful time," she replied.

"Where did he take you for lunch?"

"A private dining room at the Brighton. He had the entire room filled with flowers, Fiona. He remembered I'd written that I loved flowers."

"Hmm, too bad you didn't write that you loved diamonds."

Again Cara looked down at the ring, a ring she was wearing under false pretenses. Not only was she not the woman he thought she was, but she also had no intention of marrying him.

"So, did you tell him the truth? Did you confess your identity?"

"Not yet, although I intend to when I see him today."

"So, you're seeing him again today?"

Cara got up from the table and placed the teakettle on the stove top to heat for another cup of tea. "Yes. He called me first thing this morning and told me he'd like me to take him sightseeing."

"Sightseeing in Mission Creek? What's there to see besides cattle?"

"That's exactly what Omar wants to see," Cara explained. "He'd like me to show him around the ranch."

"Sounds wonderfully boring," Fiona replied.

"It won't be boring. Not with Omar there."

There was a long pause. "It sounds like you like

him, Cara. Are you sure you really want to tell him the truth today?"

Cara sighed. "No, I don't want to tell him the truth today, and yes, I do like him." She thought of that kiss…the kiss that had rocked her to her very core. "I like him a lot."

"Then, don't be in such a big hurry to tell him the truth. It's not like you're breaking any law, Cara. You can even borrow some of my clothes, if you want to keep up the pretense until the sheik goes back home."

"Thanks. I'll think about it," Cara replied, although she had no intention of continuing the fabrication.

"Well, sis, I've got to run. I'm meeting some friends in just a little while. I'll keep in touch to see how this little drama plays out."

The two sisters said their goodbyes, then Cara hung up. She had to tell Omar the truth. Spending time with him the day before had been wonderful. And that kiss…oh, that kiss. Although it had been far too brief, Cara had never been kissed so thoroughly.

Even now, thinking of his lips on hers, remembering the mastery of those strong yet gentle lips, heat swirled inside her, making her almost light-headed.

A shrill whistle pulled her from her thoughts, and she quickly moved the shrieking teakettle off the burner and poured the water into her waiting cup.

She had to tell him the truth. It wasn't fair to keep fooling him. She carried her cup to the table and sank down once again. But was it so awful to wait another day or two?

After all, several times the day before he'd mentioned something about her letters. He'd told her that he'd seen her intelligence and sensitivity in those written pages. And those letters he'd referred to had been written by her, not by Fiona.

What was the harm in waiting just another couple of days, spending a little more time with him and making him realize she—Elizabeth Cara Carson— was the woman he wanted, the woman he needed as his wife?

Frowning, she took a sip of her tea. What was she thinking? It wasn't as if she actually wanted to marry Omar. She just wanted to be the woman *he wanted* to marry.

She finished her tea, then decided to take advantage of Fiona's generous offer to loan her clothes. Cara suddenly had a desire to be more colorful, more stylish, more exciting for Omar, and she certainly wasn't going to find anything suitable in her own closet.

She rinsed her cup and put it in the dishwasher, then left the cottage and headed for the big house.

It was a beautiful November day: The sun was bright and the temperature was a moderate seventy degrees. The climate, the foliage and the ranch animals were all as familiar to Cara as her own heartbeat.

She'd been born here on the Carson ranch and raised by her parents, Grace and Ford. For all her twenty-seven years she'd been completely happy here. She'd been surrounded not only by the love of her family, but also by the beautiful land that had made them prosperous.

But in the past year she'd felt a growing, vague sense of dissatisfaction, a dissatisfaction that had exploded into utter unhappiness three days before the last school year ended.

She hungered for something new...something different. She was tired of Texas and the predictable life she had built for herself.

She entered the house, grateful that she didn't encounter anyone as she made her way up the stairway and toward Fiona's suite of rooms.

It was obvious that Fiona had packed in a hurry for her impromptu trip to Paris. Clothes were strewn on top of the unmade bed and across a chair, and Cara knew it wouldn't be long before one of the maids came in to make sense out of the disorder her sister had left behind.

She went directly to the huge walk-in closet and eyed the selection. There was no doubt about it, Fiona was a clotheshorse. Formals, tea-length dresses, riding habits and sportswear—she had clothing for every occasion imaginable.

It took Cara only a few minutes to choose several casual outfits and two more formal dresses; then, with the clothing in her arms, she headed out of the bedroom.

"Fiona?"

Her mother's familiar voice stopped Cara in her tracks. She turned, and her mother smiled.

"Oh, Cara, it's you. I thought for a moment your sister had cut short her trip."

"No, I just decided to borrow a few of her things. She called me this morning and told me it would be all right for me to wear some of her clothes."

Grace Carson looked far too young to be the mother not only of twenty-seven-year-old twins, but also the mother of two strapping sons in their thirties, Matt and Flynt.

She now eyed her daughter curiously. "I've never known you to be particularly interested in borrowing your sister's clothing," she observed.

"I just felt like something different…something a little more colorful, a little more stylish than what I normally wear."

Grace held Cara's gaze and crossed her arms over her plump chest. "Does this have anything to do with the male species? Usually when a woman has her hair restyled or buys new clothes, it means a new man in her life."

Cara hesitated. "It's Sheik Omar Al Abdar," she blurted out, as a blush heated her cheeks. "I hadn't mentioned it before, but for the past year he and I have been writing each other. He arrived in town yesterday to see me."

Grace smiled. "That's wonderful, dear. You spend far too much time cooped up in that cottage. Be sure to bring him around to see your father and me. We'll show him some of our famous Texan hospitality."

"Mother…" Cara began. "The sheik…he's very

formal. He calls me Elizabeth, and I would appreciate it if you and Daddy would call me Elizabeth when you're in his presence."

A frown tugged at Grace's plump, pretty features, and once again she studied Cara. "I'm not going to ask questions, Cara. You're an adult and I trust your judgment, but…"

She *knew.* Somehow Cara's mother knew something wasn't quite right. "Everything is fine," Cara assured her. "I know what I'm doing."

*Of course, I really have no idea what I'm doing,* Cara thought a moment later as she left the main house and headed back to her cottage.

All she knew was that somehow she'd already made the decision to give herself more time… Just a little more time. Then she'd tell Omar the truth.

Omar handed Rashad his suit jacket just before he and Elizabeth were set to take off for their walk around Carson Ranch.

It was just after noon and the sun overhead was bright and beat warmly on his broad shoulders, but he noticed only how it played in her hair, teasing out impish tones of red and gold in the dark brown strands.

"Rashad will wait here with the car where there is a phone," he said to her, then frowned apologetically. "I'm afraid that my negotiations are at a crisis stage and I cannot be away from a phone for too long."

Elizabeth nodded and smiled at Omar's aide.

"Rashad, if you or the others get thirsty or anything, please feel free to go into the cottage and help yourself." The "others" were the driver of the car and two bodyguards.

Rashad gave a formal bow. "Your hospitality is most appreciated, but I will be fine here."

"Shall we begin the tour?" Omar asked as he took her hand in his. He smiled at her. "Although I would be just as content to stand here and look at you all day long. You look like a piece of sunshine."

He was granted one of her beautiful smiles. "Thank you," she replied.

It was true. Wearing yellow slacks and a matching blouse, she looked beautifully vibrant. The bright color emphasized the richness of her dark hair, and the cut of the clothes complemented her shapeliness.

"I don't wear yellow very often," she explained as they began walking away from her cottage.

"You should. It becomes you. I'll see to it that you have a dozen outfits in that color when we are married."

Her eyes seemed to flirt with him as she cast him a sideways glance. "You're very sure of yourself, considering the fact that I haven't agreed to marry you yet."

"Ah, but you will." He squeezed her hand lightly. "I will see to it that you find me utterly irresistible. There are women in Gaspar that find me so."

She eyed him again, her eyes twinkling. "Perhaps they have lower standards than I do."

He laughed, delighted that she could not only meet his wit, but challenge it, as well. "Then, for you, I will simply try harder."

As they walked toward the outbuildings in the distance, Elizabeth shot a quick glance behind them. "Do they go everywhere that you do?" she asked.

He knew she was speaking of the bodyguards who followed behind them at a discreet distance. "I am only without them when I am in my private quarters in Gaspar. That is one of the things you would have to become accustomed to as my wife—the presence of guards in your life."

She nodded thoughtfully. "I'm sure life in Gaspar would be far different from life here in Texas." She pulled her hand from his in order to open a gate that led to a pasture.

As they walked through the lush green grass dotted with wildflowers, she shared with him some of the history of the ranch.

He listened with interest as she explained to him about Big Bill Carson and J. P. Wainwright, who had met on a cattle-buying trip in 1898 and become good friends. In 1923 the two families had founded the Lone Star Country Club.

When the large herd of cattle came into view, Omar was surprised at how knowledgeable she was about the breeding, buying and selling process.

While he found the conversation interesting, far more fascinating to him were the expressions on her lovely face as she spoke. She had a face made for storytelling, expressive and animated. It was easy for him to imagine her entertaining their children with stories of her days in the faraway land of Texas.

"I'll bet you were a wonderful teacher," he said, as they paused to rest for a few minutes in the shade of a small grove of trees.

"Why do you say that?" She leaned with her back against a tree trunk.

Omar stood directly in front of her and braced himself with a hand on the trunk next to her head. "Your face lights up when you speak of things you care about. You must have generated a lot of enthusiasm among your students."

"I liked teaching." Shadows momentarily doused the light in her eyes.

He fought the impulse to reach out and stroke the shiny length of her hair. Instead he eyed her curiously. "You never told me why you decided to take some time off from your teaching position."

A frown creased her delicate forehead, and she gazed off into the distance. When she finally looked at him once again, the shadows in her eyes were deeper, darker.

"It was three days before the end of the school year," she finally said. "The bell had just rung for the end of the last class of the day, and the students were all leaving the building. I was gathering up my things, also getting ready to head home, when Donny Albright burst into my room."

She paused, and once again looked off into the distance. "And who is Donny Albright?" Omar asked.

She sighed, a deep, tremulous sigh that made Omar want to sweep her up into his arms and hold her against his chest. At the moment she looked achingly vulnerable.

"He was a senior, a troubled young man. But until that day none of us realized just how troubled he was." She reached up and tucked a strand of her hair behind her ear. "Anyway, when he came into the room, he was distraught, crying and yelling so that I couldn't understand what was wrong. I finally managed to get out of him that he'd failed his math class and wasn't going to graduate."

She pushed herself away from the tree trunk and gestured to Omar that she wanted to walk once again. He grabbed one of her hands, surprised to find it bone cold and trembling slightly. "What happened?"

"Donny wanted me to speak to Mr. McNair, his math teacher. He wanted me to get McNair to change his final grade. When I told Donny I couldn't do that, he pulled out a gun. He held me at gunpoint for three hours before I finally talked him into giving up to the police, who by then had surrounded the building."

Horror shot through Omar, and he halted in his tracks, drew her against his chest and wrapped his arms around her. He couldn't imagine the terror she must have gone through.

She leaned into his embrace, as if gathering strength from his arms. The clean scent of her hair

filled his senses, and he tried not to focus on the evoc-
ative sensation of her warm breasts pressed against
his chest.

"You must have been terrified," he murmured as
he ran a hand up and down her slender back.

She sighed once again, then stepped back from
him, and they continued to walk. "It's funny, I wasn't
frightened while it was all happening. I never believed
Donny would actually shoot me. What I worried about
more was Donny getting hurt by the police."

The fact that she had been concerned for the boy
impressed Omar. "If that had happened to you in
Gaspar, I would have thrown the boy into a dungeon."

"Do you have dungeons in Gaspar?" she asked.

"No, but I would build one specifically for people
who threatened the safety of what belongs to me, for
people who would attempt to harm you."

Her eyes brightened, and she smiled at him. "While
I don't necessarily approve of the method, I appreciate
the sentiment." Her smile fell away. "Besides, Donny
didn't need a dungeon. He needed help. We learned
later that both his parents were severe alcoholics and
that Donny had spent the previous two years raising
his three younger sisters. He was frantic about his di-
ploma because he was certain without it he wouldn't
be able to get a good job, and he was trying to save
up enough money to take his sisters and leave his parents."

"A sad affair," he replied. "However, I can understand why you were reluctant to return to the school."

"Actually, I returned the next day and finished out the school year and thought I was fine." Again the shadows appeared in her eyes.

"But you weren't fine."

She shook her head, dark strands flying on either side of her heart-shaped face. "I think for a couple of days I was kind of in shock, then I started having nightmares about the whole thing. The nightmares don't come as often anymore, just occasionally. But I made the decision that I didn't want to go back this year."

"I don't blame you. I'm sure the idea of entering that building again must be difficult."

"That isn't why I decided not to go back."

He looked at her in surprise. "Then, why?"

She waited until they had left the pasture and she'd carefully locked the gate behind them before she replied.

"I think that whole incident with Donny made me realize just how short life is, that it can be taken away from you in the snap of a finger. I just decided I wanted to take some time off and enjoy life to the fullest."

"Ah, so what you seek is a confirmation of life," he observed.

"Yes, something like that," she agreed.

He grinned at her teasingly. "They say the best way of doing that is to make love."

Her cheeks warmed with sweet color. "I wouldn't know about that."

He looked at her in surprise. "You have never made love?" he asked incredulously.

She raised her chin. "Well, it certainly hasn't been from lack of opportunity," she exclaimed defensively.

"I wouldn't have dreamed anything to the contrary," he replied with amusement. "I just assumed in this day and age that you had enjoyed an intimate relationship before."

They had almost reached the cottage, where his car was parked out front. "I guess I'm more old-fashioned than I pretend. Besides, I simply haven't met the right man," she said.

Omar pulled her into his arms once again, enjoying the way her eyes flared in surprise. "You have met him now, Elizabeth. I will be the man who will introduce you to the pleasures of making love."

"Omar..."

Whatever she was about to say was drowned out by Rashad yelling his name and holding up the phone. Omar frowned, torn between his desire to spend more time with Elizabeth and the duty that called him yet again.

"I must take that," he said. "Rashad would not have called me if it wasn't an important call."

She nodded, and he hurried to where Rashad stood and took the cell phone. The call required Omar to return to his hotel room, where he had the paperwork required to deal with the problem. He hung up the phone and went back to where Elizabeth waited.

"I am so sorry," he said. "I'm afraid I must return to the hotel room to attend to some business."

"Of course, I understand," she said, but he thought he saw a whisper of disappointment in her eyes. He leaned forward and pressed his lips to her forehead. "Dine with me tonight?"

"I'd love to," she replied.

"Good, then I will send the car for you around seven."

"I'll be ready."

How he wanted to gather her back into his arms and taste the sweetness of her lips. But he knew now was not the time or the place.

"She is perfect," he said to Rashad moments later, when they were driving back to the hotel. "She is perfect, just like I knew she would be. I have made a wise and good choice."

He stared out the window, thinking of the woman he'd just left, then looked back at Rashad. "She is intelligent and sensitive and has a compassion inside her that will make her valuable not only to me as a man, but to my country as my queen."

"And it doesn't hurt that she is not hard to look at," Rashad said slyly.

Omar grinned at his assistant and friend. "No, that certainly doesn't hurt."

He redirected his gaze out the window, his thoughts once again filled with Elizabeth. He liked her even more than he'd thought he would. He'd known from her letters that there were many things he admired, but he hadn't expected to enjoy her company quite as much as he did.

Of course, his feelings for her would never deepen into anything remotely resembling love. His father, Sheik Abdul Al Abdar, had warned him from an early age that love took away a man's power, made him look dependent and weak in the eyes of his countrymen.

Love was out of the question—but desire certainly wasn't, and the thought that Elizabeth had never been with a man before stirred Omar with anticipation.

If he could seduce her tonight, he had a feeling she would easily succumb to his wishes that she marry him.

He leaned back in his seat and closed his eyes, planning the seduction of the lovely Elizabeth Fiona Carson.

In a jungle in a rain forest in the Central American country of Mezcaya, Luke Callaghan leaned his head back against a tree trunk, closed his eyes and for a moment imagined he was back home in Texas.

The sound of distant gunfire, the buzz of the infernal mosquitoes and the exhausting humidity seemed to fade away as he thought of home.

Luke had grown up on an estate twenty miles north of Mission Creek. Orphaned at seven, he'd been left an amount of money that made him a millionaire many times over, but he'd never cared much about the money.

The military had provided the family Luke had

wanted, and now at the age of thirty-four he had achieved his desire. He was a double agent, working for the military in a position so secretive even his best friends didn't know about it.

He smiled grimly and raked a hand over his jaw as he thought of his buddies back home.

They would all probably think he was off on another party jaunt, wining and dining women all over the world. None of them would believe that he was in a stinking jungle fighting terrorists.

His mouth watered as he thought of a rack of ribs dripping with barbecue sauce. Ribs and a cold beer—that was the first thing he'd order when he got back to Texas.

If he ever got out of this infernal jungle alive.

## Chapter 4

For the first time in her life, Cara felt just a little bit like Fiona as she stared at her reflection in the mirror. The red silk dress she'd borrowed from Fiona's closet, and now wore, made her feel flirty and sexy and desirable. Or was it Omar who made her feel that way?

She had spent the afternoon after he'd left, playing and replaying in her mind the entire time with him. Each time he'd looked at her with those beautiful dark eyes of his, she had felt a shiver of excitement. For in his eyes she'd seen desire.

When she'd told him about her trouble at school and he'd pulled her into his arms, she'd wanted to remain standing there forever.

His arms surrounding her had made her feel more

safe than she ever had, and for just a moment she'd thought she could hear his heartbeat against her own.

A knock on her door pulled her from her thoughts, and she whirled away from the bedroom mirror and hurried to the door, certain it must be the car to drive her to Omar.

She opened the door, surprised to see not Rashad standing on her front stoop, but her father. "Daddy!" she exclaimed in surprise.

"Hi, darlin'. Don't you look like a picture of prettiness?"

"Thank you," Cara replied, and smiled affectionately at her father.

Ford Carson was a big man, with broad shoulders, a belly that just overhung the large belt buckles he favored, and hair that had gone a snowy white in the past couple of years. Since Cara had moved into the cottage two years before, Ford often dropped in unannounced just to visit with her.

He stepped into the living room but remained standing. "I guess you're on your way out," he said. "Your mama told me Sheik Al Abdar is in town and you've been spending time with him. I hope this isn't anything too serious."

Cara looked at him in surprise. "You don't like Omar?"

"Hell, I like him fine, but I'd hate to see my little girl taken off to some foreign country, even if the country is friendly with the United States."

Cara smiled. "Daddy, I'm not a little girl anymore,

and I'm sure I could come home to visit whenever I wanted."

Ford frowned, his bushy dark eyebrows pulling together in the center of his forehead. "So, this *is* serious."

"Oh, I don't know. But I like him a lot," she replied honestly.

Ford sighed. "I always figured it would be your sister who'd eventually go off to live in some foreign place. She's never seemed satisfied in Mission Creek. But you...I just always thought you'd be around."

With a small laugh, Cara threw her arms around his neck. "I'm not gone yet," she said. "I'm just enjoying Omar's company at the moment. Don't look so worried."

Ford kissed her soundly on the cheek. "I always worry when it comes to my family."

Cara stepped back from him. "Well, you know you don't have to worry about me. I'm not about to do anything foolish or impulsive."

"I know that, honeybunch. I came by to tell you that we're planning a little barbecue tomorrow afternoon. Your brothers and their wives will be there, and I thought you might want to invite Sheik Omar. We're going to eat at about three."

"I can't give you an answer right now. We'll see what the plans are," she hedged as they stepped back out on the porch.

The last thing she wanted was for Omar to spend any time around her family and for somebody to slip and call her Cara. Until she told him the truth, the best thing to do was keep him isolated from her family. *A tangled web,* she thought to herself, wishing she'd never begun the subterfuge in the first place.

"I suppose I'd better head back to the house. Your mama will think I'm out here trying to sneak a smoke, but with that damn diet she's got me on, I'd be more apt to sneak a big juicy steak or a platter of ribs."

Cara laughed. "You know Mama just wants what's best for you."

"I know, but if I have to look at another string bean or piece of dried-up chicken breast, I just might have that heart attack everyone is so worried about." With another quick kiss to Cara's cheek, he waved, then headed back toward the main house.

Cara watched him until he was out of sight, her heart filled with love for the man who had been such an influence in her life. Fiona had been his parrot, squawky and vivid and bright. But Cara had been his sparrow, and he'd always been especially gentle and loving with her.

Her nerves went on alert as she heard the approach of a car and saw in the distance the familiar limo approaching her cottage. She raced inside and grabbed her small beaded purse, then hurried back outside.

"Good evening, Ms. Carson." Rashad greeted her with a beaming smile as he opened the door to allow her into the luxury limo.

"Good evening, Rashad," she replied. She climbed into the backseat, then leaned forward. "I would be pleased to have your company back here for the ride into town."

His dark eyes lit with surprise. "Thank you, I would enjoy sharing your company." He got into the back with her and sat opposite her, with his back to the driver. He knocked on the window that separated the driver from them, and the limo took off.

"Are you enjoying your time in Mission Creek, Rashad?" she asked.

He nodded. "I'm finding it most interesting. Texans seem to be larger than life."

Cara laughed at the apt description, then sobered. "Have you worked for Omar a long time?"

"For many years, and for his father before him."

"Tell me about him," she said, wanting to know anything and everything about Omar, including about his family.

"Sheik Abdul Al Abdar was a good and wise ruler and much beloved by his people. There was some concern when he handed the reins to Omar on Omar's thirtieth birthday."

"Concern? About what?"

Rashad cast her an impish smile. "Sheik Omar had something of a reputation as a playboy. There were some who thought he wasn't ready, wasn't man enough to take his father's place. But he has proved the cynics wrong. He has become as beloved in Gaspar as his father before him."

He glanced at her slyly. "And the woman he marries will be as beloved as he."

"Matchmaking, Rashad?" she teased.

"But, of course." He grinned broadly. "I know how much Sheik Omar enjoyed your correspondence with him over the past year. I could always tell when he'd received a letter from you. He'd smile more on those days."

Rashad's words thrilled Cara. She'd felt the same way when she'd received Omar's letters. They had always managed to brighten her day and warm her heart.

*My words,* she thought to herself. *It was my words that he read, my words that made him happy. Not Fiona's.* Somehow this knowledge made her impersonation of her twin seem less dishonest.

She was still feeling the glow of pleasure when the limo pulled up outside the Brighton Hotel. Rashad saw her out, but instead of escorting her to the same dining room where they had eaten the night before, he led her to the elevator.

"Sheik Omar has made arrangements to dine in his suite this evening," he explained as they stepped into the awaiting elevator.

*His suite.* Complete privacy. Cara felt a shiver of anticipation. It would be a perfect opportunity for her to confess her secret to him.

She gazed down at the ring on her finger. Though telling him was the right thing to do, she had a feeling it would end their time together.

Heaven help her, she wasn't ready for that.

When they reached the eighth floor, they got out

of the elevator and walked down a hallway to another elevator.

Rashad used a key and the doors shooshed open. "I will leave you now," he said with a small bow. "This elevator will take you directly to Sheik Omar's suite."

"Thank you, Rashad." She stepped into the elevator, and the doors closed.

She smoothed her hands down her dress, suddenly worried that perhaps the flirty, sexy red dress was a bit much. She should have worn basic black. Somehow she felt that it would be easier to tell him the truth if she were dressed like herself, instead of like her sister.

The elevator came to a halt, the doors opened, and Omar stood before her. The red dress was the right choice, she immediately thought as she saw the glittering fires that ignited in his eyes.

"Elizabeth, you take my breath away with your beauty," he said as he took her hand and led her out of the elevator.

"You take my breath away," she replied. She had never before seen him dressed in his traditional Middle Eastern clothing.

He wore an elegant silk floor-length white robe that emphasized the sun-darkened tones of his olive skin. A turban encrusted with brilliant jewels hid his hair, but brought attention to his bold, handsome facial features.

He looked foreign and mysterious—until he smiled, and then he simply looked like Omar, the man who was precariously close to winning her heart.

"Please, come in." He gestured toward the over-stuffed white sofa. "Dinner will not be served for a little while. Would you care for a glass of wine?"

"That would be nice," she replied as she sat on the sofa and looked around the room with interest. It was a large living area done all in pristine whites and rich golds.

A small alcove provided an intimate area for dining. The table was set with white china and sparkling crystal, and a centerpiece of half a dozen candles.

A door was open to the bedroom, the luxurious king-size bed visible from where she sat. The bedroom was dimly lit, and she could see that the bed had been turned down as if in anticipation of someone sliding between the sheets.

For just a moment her mind granted her a vision of her and Omar beneath the white sheets, his large hands stroking down the length of her as his lips plied hers with heat. Her pulse leaped in response, and she quickly shoved the image away.

Exotic music played softly—an orchestra of lutes, triangles, cymbals and other instruments she didn't recognize. She knew it must be music from his country, and she felt as if he were attempting to seduce her with pieces of Gaspar.

As he handed her the glass of wine, his fingers lingered momentarily on hers, the touch shooting electric currents up her arm. "Thank you," she murmured breathlessly.

"You're welcome." He sat next to her, his dark eyes lingering on her. She could smell him, the scent of mysterious spices and masculinity, a scent that stirred her senses.

"You look more stunning tonight than you did six years ago at the cotillion," he said. He reached out and touched a strand of her hair, as if unable to stop himself from making some sort of physical contact.

"And you look quite majestic," she replied. She took a drink of her wine. "I've never seen you dressed like a sheik."

He laughed. "And just how does a sheik dress?"

"In long silk robes and jeweled turbans."

He dropped his hand from her hair and leaned back, his dark eyes holding the same smile that his lips formed. "Actually, few sheiks in this day and age cling to the traditional clothing. Most wear suits and shirts and have their feet firmly planted in the modern world."

"Then, you are not quite a modern sheik?" she asked.

"My father sent me to a private school in England, then university in Paris, and finally business school in New York City. He wanted me to experience the world, learn the modern ways and bring them back to my country so that Gaspar would continue to prosper. But he also taught me the importance of tradition. Besides," he said, his smile widening, "the traditional clothes are extremely comfortable."

"And very attractive," she added, then quickly

took another sip of her wine. She was slightly overwhelmed, not only by the romantic setting, but by Omar's dark handsomeness and the glow that flamed in his beautiful eyes each time he looked at her.

She'd thought it was the dress that made her feel sexy and desirable, but she realized now it was him. Each time he looked at her she felt unbelievably beautiful. It was a heady, wonderful feeling.

"I enjoyed seeing the ranch this afternoon. It's an impressive spread."

"It was a wonderful place to grow up," she replied, relaxing slightly as the conversation turned to her birthplace. "There were always people around. Not only the ranch hands, but we often had a houseful of guests. There's nothing that my father loves more than to smoke a mess of ribs and have a huge barbecue."

She thought of the barbecue her father had mentioned earlier. She was supposed to invite Omar, but she was torn. She knew there was no way he could spend time with her two brothers and their wives and not discover that she was Cara.

But perhaps it would be best to invite him and let the chips fall where they may. "In fact, my father stopped by the cottage right before the car came to pick me up and mentioned that he's planning a little barbecue tomorrow afternoon. He wanted to make sure I invited you to attend."

"What time?" Omar asked.

"About three."

A deep frown creased his broad forehead. "I'm

afraid I'll have to take a rain check. I've scheduled the entire afternoon tomorrow for conference calls."

Guilt swept through her as she realized the tremendous relief she felt. "How are your negotiations coming along?"

His frown deepened. "Not as well as I'd hoped." His nostrils flared slightly, and for a moment he looked positively fierce. "The men I am dealing with take me for a fool. They want me to give away our oil, but they will discover that I am not a man to compromise." He drew a deep breath and the frown disappeared. "But tonight we won't talk about business."

He picked up the bottle of wine from the coffee table and offered her some more. She held out her glass, recognizing that she had just caught a glimpse of Omar the Sheik, fierce and proud and unwilling to compromise his beliefs or his people.

He poured himself more wine, then once again settled back on the sofa. "You mentioned your brothers. Tell me about them."

"Well, Flynt just got married in June." Cara smiled as she thought of the happiness her brother had found with his new bride, Josie. "There was a time when we were all quite worried about him. Almost three years ago he lost his wife and unborn child in a car accident, and there were times we weren't sure he was going to survive the tragedy. It took a very special girl named Lena to bring him out of his sorrow."

"Lena? This is his child?"

"No, she's a baby girl who was found on the ninth

tee on the golf course at the Lone Star Country Club. It's a bizarre story. Nobody knows who the little girl is. Flynt was golfing that day with some buddies, and when they found the baby, he just knew he had to take her home. It changed his life."

"Amazing. Have they since discovered who the baby belongs to?"

She shook her head. "No, but Flynt and Josie have been taking good care of her." She smiled again, thinking of the dark-haired, blue-eyed little girl. "She's such a sweet baby. I can't imagine what would make a mother abandon a baby on a golf course, or anywhere else for that matter."

"Who knows what drives people to do what they do."

He leaned toward her, and again her senses filled with the scent of him.

"I'll bet you will make a wonderful mother."

"I hope so," she replied. "I certainly had a good role model."

"You're close to your mother?"

She nodded. "Very close, and to my father, too. They have been wonderful parents, supportive and loving."

He reached out and ran his fingers up her forearm, his touch inflaming her nerve endings.

"And that's the kind of parents we will make, supportive and loving to the many babies we will have."

She laughed shakily, finding it more and more difficult to concentrate on the conversation when his fingers were caressing her arm so sweetly. "Many babies? How many children do you have in mind?"

"As many as you would give me," he replied softly. He set his wineglass on the coffee table and with deliberate intent took hers from her hand and placed it next to his.

Her heartbeat raced as he drew her into his arms.

"I would love making babies with you, Elizabeth." He reached up and drew a hand through her hair. His strong fingers clenched, capturing the strands and he gently tugged her head back as if to give him access to her lips.

He held her gaze for just a moment, then moved to capture her mouth with his. At first, the kiss was infinitely tender and Cara's heart swelled with emotion.

The talk of babies, of making a family, had seduced her almost as effectively as the music and the candlelight. But nothing seduced her more than the gentle featherlight softness of his lips against hers.

And when he sought to deepen the kiss by using his tongue to toy first at her lips, then to swirl inside her mouth, she felt a sexual stirring within her.

She felt it first in the pit of her stomach, a burst of fire that exploded, sending heat throughout her body. Her breasts tightened, the nipples pressing against the silk of her bra. She was shocked by how her body was responding to a simple kiss—

A small buzzer sounded, and Omar reluctantly pulled his mouth from hers just as the elevator doors opened to reveal a waiter pushing a large serving trolley.

Omar stood to greet the waiter, but Elizabeth remained seated, instinctively knowing that if she tried to stand, her legs would probably buckle beneath her.

Her heart still pounded too fast, her pulse raced in an abnormal rhythm and the surface of her skin felt feverish. She picked up her wineglass and took a full gulp, hoping the chilled white wine would douse the fire Omar's kiss had lit inside her.

By the time the meal had been placed on the table and the waiter had departed, Cara felt more in control of herself. She sat in the chair that Omar held out for her, shivering slightly as his hands lingered for a moment too long on her shoulders.

"I hope the food is good," he said as he sat next to her, "because the timing of its arrival was rotten."

She smiled, picked up the linen napkin and placed it on her lap. "It could have been worse. The food might have arrived fifteen minutes later—and it would have been more embarrassing."

His eyes fired with a hunger that had nothing to do with the food before them. "Perhaps there won't be any need to order dessert."

"We'll see," she replied with a small smile. "Although, it would take something magnificent to make me forget the pleasure of chocolate."

She was teasing, flirting with him, and it amazed her. She'd rarely found the confidence it took to tease a man.

His dark brows lifted and his eyes twinkled. "I can promise you, what I have in mind is far more pleasurable than mere chocolate."

Cara believed him, and felt a new shiver of anticipation. Suddenly, chocolate was the last thing on her mind.

The moment she'd walked out of the elevator, Omar had wanted to sweep her up in his arms, carry her into the bedroom and pull the delightfully sexy red dress right off her body.

Although, the dress did amazing things to her. The cinched waist made her look slender, but emphasized the thrust of her breasts. The short, full skirt drew attention to the long length of her shapely legs, and Omar wanted nothing more than to trail his fingers up them. He had a feeling her skin would be silky soft and sweetly perfumed.

Now, as they ate their meal of leg of lamb and parsleyed new potatoes, he watched her covetously. Each movement of her lips as she ate heightened the desire that had been thrumming inside him.

"I believe we got sidetracked when we were discussing your brothers," he said, trying to take his mind off how much he wanted to make love to her, how much he wanted to be the man to introduce her to the pleasure of physical intimacy.

"You told me about Flynt, but you mentioned another brother, as well."

"Yes, Matt." She dabbed her lush lips with the

napkin, then paused to take a sip of her water. "He shocked the entire family in July by marrying Rose Wainwright."

"Why is that shocking?" he asked curiously.

"Because for years there has been a long-standing feud between the Wainwrights and the Carsons."

Omar knew the Wainwright family, like the Carsons, was one of the most powerful families in the state of Texas. He also knew it had been the Wainwrights and the Carsons who had founded the luxury Lone Star Country Club.

"Hopefully this isn't a Romeo and Juliet kind of story."

She smiled. "Not at all. They are extremely happy together, but unfortunately their marriage hasn't really brought the families together. It was more just a temporary truce."

"That's too bad—but you're close to your family." It was an observation rather than a question.

"Yes, I am." She took another drink of her water, her dainty pink tongue licking her upper lip when she was finished. "We've always been a close-knit family."

By the time the meal was finished, Omar felt as if he'd been simmering for the past two hours and was on the verge of a full boil. He couldn't remember the last time he'd felt such intense desire for a woman. Nor could he remember feeling this much concern that he might not be successful in his seduction.

While he saw the promise of fire in her eyes, he

knew she hadn't remained a virgin this long by allowing herself to burn.

After the meal they returned to the sofa where Omar served them after-dinner liqueur coffee. "Hmm, this is wonderful," she said as she licked a dollop of whipped cream from the corner of her mouth. "What's in it?"

"A little crème de cacao, brandy, Kahlúa, coffee and whipped cream. You like it?"

"It's positively decadent." She took another sip and again the whipped cream clung to her upper lip. Before she could lick it off, he reached out and dragged his index finger across the creamy substance.

His heart crashed into his ribs as she grabbed his wrist and sucked his finger into her mouth, her green eyes never leaving his. He pulled his finger away and hungrily covered her lips with his own. Blood seemed to surge through every vein in his body.

Her mouth tasted of coffee and Kahlúa, a bittersweet combination that drove him half mad with desire. He was vaguely aware of her reaching to set her mug down on the coffee table, and he broke the kiss only long enough to allow her to do so.

When he reached for her again, he pulled her against his chest and claimed her mouth with his, wanting to possess her, body and soul.

She responded with a hunger that surprised him. She wound her arms around his neck and pressed herself against his chest.

He leaned back, dragging her with him so that she

was on top of him. His hands caressed up and down her back, enjoying the feel of her warm skin beneath the silky dress.

As his hands moved lower, down into the small of her back, just above the sweet curve of her buttocks, she gasped against his mouth.

The gasp ignited him with want, with the need to further explore her mysteries. He'd begun the evening with a calculated plan to seduce her into marrying him, but now was rapidly losing control.

His hands moved from her back, lingering at her sides where the swell of her breasts began. Still their mouths sought each other's with hunger. When his hands covered her breasts, a tiny moan escaped her, a moan of pleasure that electrified him.

He tore his mouth from hers and gazed at her, noting that her eyes were deep, deep green and filled with the haze of sexual excitement. "I want you, Elizabeth. I want to take you to my bed and make love to you."

"I want you, too," she replied, her lips quivering slightly. She pushed off his chest and sat up. "But I don't want to make love with you unless it's on our wedding night."

Omar straightened, as well, triumph soaring through him. "Then, you will marry me?"

Her lips trembled for a moment before she answered. "Yes," she said softly.

He grabbed her hand and raised it to his lips. "You have made me a happy man," he said, then kissed the back of her hand. "We'll get the license tomorrow, then marry as soon as possible."

"Not as soon as possible," she protested. "I'll need some time…"

Omar frowned. "Time for what?"

She worried a hand through her hair. "I don't know, I've never gotten married before. I'd like some time to make the arrangements and to pick out the perfect wedding gown. This will be my one and only wedding and I'd like it to be a special memory."

Her sentimentality only assured him that she was the right choice for his wife. "How about a month?" Although he would have preferred a wedding as soon as possible, he would not deny her the pleasure of being a bride-to-be for a month. And he would do whatever he could to remain in the States for the next thirty days.

"All right." She gave him a beatific smile. "Then, I guess we'll get married right after Thanksgiving."

He pulled her into his arms once again. "And I will give thanks for the rest of my life that fate brought you into my life."

He started to kiss her again, but she stopped him with a finger over his lips. "Omar, I don't think we should do any more kissing tonight. In fact, I think I should go home." She held his gaze with somber eyes. "I'm feeling fairly vulnerable right now, and I really want our wedding night to be special."

Her candor enchanted him, and although he would have loved to have her at that very moment, he abided by her wishes and stood. "I'll summon Rashad with the car."

As he picked up the phone, he watched her stand and straighten her dress. Her lips were slightly swollen from the kisses they'd indulged in, and her skin glowed with a radiance that was bewitching.

He thought of that night at the cotillion so long ago. He, along with every other man at the dance, had coveted the dazzling, beautiful, flirtatious Elizabeth, and he couldn't help but be pleased that he was the man who had captured her.

Cara sat in the back of the limo carrying her away from the hotel and back to her cottage. She couldn't believe she'd just agreed to marry Omar.

It hadn't been her intention to agree to his marriage proposal, but his lips had been so hot on hers. His hands had been so masterful as they stroked along her skin. Rational thought had fled beneath his sensual onslaught and she had fallen into the sweet promise in his eyes.

Even though she hadn't intended to accept, she couldn't help the wave of joy that fluttered through her. She was officially engaged to a handsome sheik, a man who caused her pulse to race and her heart to warm.

She didn't want to think about all the reasons why she shouldn't be engaged to him. As the limo pulled up before her little cottage, she decided that just for tonight she would wrap her happiness around her and worry about tomorrow...tomorrow.

"There's a butt pincher at table seven," Haley fumed to Ginger as the two met in the kitchen to pick up orders. They were both working in the Men's Grill that evening, and the night had not started well for Haley.

As always, she was wired by the FBI, who hoped she would overhear something, anything that would benefit them in their investigation into the mob's smuggling operation.

She was always nervous when working in the Men's Grill, knowing that she was wired and playing a dangerous game.

Tonight her nerves seemed more jangled than usual. She'd spilled a drink on the first person she'd served, and mixed up another order. Now, having had her butt pinched three times so far by the creep at table seven, she was ready to walk out.

"There's nothing worse than a butt pincher," Ginger said sympathetically, then grinned. "Unless it's a breast brusher."

Despite her irritation, Haley laughed as she loaded up her order on a tray. "Ah, the perils of waitressing."

"Daisy."

Haley turned to see Harvey Small hurrying toward her, a worried frown between his beady little eyes. "What?" she asked.

"Put your tray down. Meagan is going to cover

your tables. I need you to bartend for a party in the blue dining room."

"Now?" she asked. Usually the private dining rooms were booked far in advance, and she hadn't heard of any private party being booked.

"Yeah, now. Somebody called a few minutes ago and said they'd be here in fifteen minutes. I don't even know if the bar is stocked, so you'd better hustle in there and get things ready."

"All right." She put her tray down and, with a wave to Ginger, hurried from the kitchen and headed toward what the help called the Blue Room.

The private dining room was small and decorated in navy blue. Its single table seated eight people, but could accommodate twelve. There was a built-in bar against one wall, and Haley went directly there to make certain everything she would need for serving drinks was stocked.

She didn't mind working the private rooms. Not only was there an automatic gratuity built into the patrons' checks for the bartender, but usually the private parties tipped well.

And she needed the tips.

It was ironic that she'd been raised in wealth, had never wanted for anything, and for all she knew there was still a bank account somewhere with her name on it, but a dead woman couldn't access funds. And as far as everyone was concerned, Haley Mercado drowned in a lake many years ago.

*Long live Daisy Parker,* she thought bitterly.

While she waited for the party to arrive, she opened a jar of olives and another of cherries, and sliced several limes and lemons, ready for whatever drinks they might order.

She heard them before they entered, the sounds of gruff male voices and the higher-pitched voice of Harvey as he greeted them outside the door.

Then the first of the party walked in, and her breath caught painfully in her chest. Her father and her brother. For a moment, fear of being recognized was overwhelmed by the need to run to them, throw herself in their arms and weep.

This was what she'd both yearned for and feared. She'd hungered to see her family again, but knew that if they recognized her, if they discovered she was alive and well, then all she had worked for would be destroyed and her very life would be in danger.

She drew several deep breaths to steady herself, and watched as her father and brother sat at the table. She could only hope that with her now-blond hair and the plastic surgery she'd had many years ago nobody would recognize her.

Still, she drank in the sight of her father. She hadn't seen him since before her mother's death and she was vaguely surprised by how much he'd aged. His once dark, lustrous hair was almost completely gray and his hazel eyes held a sadness that broke Haley's heart.

Ricky was as handsome as ever, and more than anything, Haley wished she could hug the brother she'd grown up idolizing.

She turned and faced the wall of bottles behind her, needing to get her emotions under control. Tears burned hot against her eyes and a ball of emotion pressed heavily in her chest. She had never felt so alone in her life.

She could only remember feeling like this one other time and that had been when she'd posed as a nun to get into the hospital to see her mother after Isadora Mercado had been beaten by thugs. Thugs she suspected had been hired by one particular member of the family.

That night, after she'd tearfully revealed herself to her dying mother, she'd gone to the Saddlebag. At the popular bar she had made the mistake that set in motion the chain of events that led her here, to the Lone Star Country Club, working in disguise and wearing a wire for the FBI.

More male voices joined those of her father and brother, and she turned around to see several other "family" members arriving. Included in the group was one man who made her blood run cold—Frank Del Brio, the man she believed had hired the thugs that had killed her mother.

The tall, muscular, short-haired man swaggered into the room as if he were already head of "the family." Her engagement to Frank had prompted her to fake her own death. That and the fact that she wanted out of the Mafia family. Even in the brief time they had been engaged, she had sensed his ruthless nature, been repelled by his blind ambition and had seen his explosive temper.

To her relief, it was her brother who approached the bar. He flashed her a quick smile, his gaze shooting to her name tag. "Hi, Daisy. Why don't you set us up with two Scotch and sodas, a Scotch on the rocks, and a couple of gin and tonics."

"Coming right up," she said with a thick Texan twang.

Minutes later, as she served the drinks, she relaxed. None of the men paid her any attention. It would appear that her disguise was successful. Now all she could do was pray that at this meeting the men would discuss enough business that the FBI could make the arrests they wanted. Then Haley could claim back her life.

# Chapter 5

"A month?" Grace Carson stared at her daughter in disbelief. "You can't get married in a month! It will take at least that long just for me to get together an appropriate guest list."

The two women were seated in the sunroom just off the kitchen, where Cara had found her mother having a late-morning cup of coffee. "We don't want a big wedding, Mother," Cara protested.

Again that morning, as she and Omar had driven to City Hall to get a marriage license, she'd tried to find a way to tell him that she was Elizabeth Cara, not Elizabeth Fiona. But he'd spent most of the time on the telephone, and for the few minutes they'd had to talk, she hadn't been able to find the right words to confess.

She told herself that before the wedding she would certainly find the right time and place to tell him the truth. After all, she had a full month. However, each time she thought of confessing, her heart bucked and kicked in protest.

"Even a small wedding takes time and planning," Grace exclaimed, pulling Cara back to the moment at hand. "We'll have the ceremony at the Lone Star Country Club, of course, and a beautiful reception afterward. We'll get Ramon to do the flowers. He does such nice work. Have you thought about colors, Cara? And how many bridesmaids should you have? Oh, and what about the cake? Whom should we hire to do the cake?"

"Mother, please, take a breath," Cara exclaimed, her own head spinning with all the details her mother had brought up.

Grace paused, then laughed. "I guess I do need to take a breath, don't I?" She leaned forward in her chair and covered Cara's hand with hers, her expression suddenly serious. "Are you sure about all this? Do you really love him, Cara?"

"I do," she replied softly. And that was the problem. She had fallen in love; first with the man who had written the beautiful letters she had bundled and tied with pink ribbon and kept next to her bed.

In the past couple of days since spending time with Omar, her love for him had grown. He was tender yet passionate, intelligent yet sensitive. He stirred her not only on a physical level, but on an emotional level.

He made her feel special and exciting and wanted, and she was so afraid of losing that, of losing him.

"It's quite a challenge you have ahead," Grace said as she sat back in her chair and wrapped her plump fingers around her coffee mug.

"What do you mean?" Cara asked curiously.

"You're going to go live in a foreign country, with new people and new customs. You'll be going there as a wife to a man you haven't spent much time with. Are you sure this is really what you want?"

Cara paused and took a sip of her coffee, then smiled at her mother. "I feel as if all these years I've been living a practice run for real life, and now suddenly I'm about to begin living for the first time."

Grace looked at her with empathy. "Your sister is a difficult act to follow."

Cara laughed. "That's putting it mildly." Her burst of laughter faded and she frowned thoughtfully. "You know I adore Fiona, but Mission Creek has never been big enough to allow both of us to shine. Omar looks at me, and I feel as if I'm the most unique, special woman in the world. More than anything, I want to build a life with him in Gaspar."

Once again Grace reached out and took Cara's hand in hers. She squeezed it and smiled. "You know your daddy and I only want happiness for you. And if your happiness lies in Gaspar with Omar, then, you know you have our blessing."

Cara rose and kissed her mother on the cheek. "I

know, and thank you. And now I'm going to change and get ready for the barbecue."

That afternoon, the barbecue turned into an engagement party of sorts for Cara. Her sisters-in-law, Josie and Rose, *ooh*ed and *aah*ed over her ring and teased her about finding a handsome sheik who was sweeping her off to live in a desert palace.

It was near dusk and the barbecue was winding down when Cara carried her glass to the kitchen and found Josie sitting at the table with a tall glass of milk. Baby Lena was in a stroller next to her, sound asleep.

Cara placed her glass in the dishwasher, then joined Josie at the table. "How are you feeling?" she asked.

Josie smiled and rubbed her pregnant tummy. "We're doing just fine."

"It must be so exciting to know that in a few months you're going to have a new baby," Cara said. Her heart expanded as she thought of carrying Omar's child inside her. What a wonderful miracle that would be.

"It is," Josie agreed, then looked down at the sleeping Lena. "Loving this baby inside me makes me wonder what on earth could possess her mother to abandon her." She looked back at Cara and smiled. "But talk about exciting! I can't believe you're going to marry Sheik Al Abdar and fly off to Gaspar to live."

"He thinks I'm Fiona." The words fell from Cara's mouth before she even knew she was going to confess her secret to Josie.

"What?" Josie leaned forward in her chair and eyed her with surprise.

Suddenly Cara wanted, needed to talk to somebody about the whole mess. She quickly explained to Josie about Omar being drawn to Fiona the night of the cotillion, and writing letters to Fiona for a year.

She told her pretty blond sister-in-law that Fiona had quickly tired of the correspondence and that Cara had taken over, answering each of the sheik's letters as if she was her sister.

"Needless to say I was shocked when he showed up on my doorstep with a marriage proposal," she said.

"So he still thinks you're Fiona?" Josie asked. "How is that possible? Does he call you Fiona?"

Cara shook her head. "I signed the letters Elizabeth, and that's what he calls me. And now I'm afraid to tell him the truth."

"Why? It's obvious he was quite taken with your letters, enough so that he decided to ask you to marry him."

Cara sighed. "He's also quite taken with the memory of Fiona that night at the cotillion, and I'm not sure who he's in love with—the woman who flirted and danced with every man at that dance, or the woman who wrote the letters. I love him, Josie, and I'm scared to death that if I tell him the truth I'll lose him."

"So, what are you going to do?"

She bit her lip. "I have a month before the wedding to tell him. I keep thinking that the more time we spend together, the better he'll take it when I finally tell him the truth. I'm hoping I can make him forget about the woman at the dance that night, and that he'll realize it's me—Cara—that he loves."

Josie reached out, grabbed Cara's hand and gave it a squeeze. "I hope it works out the way you want it to, Cara. Honestly, I've never seen you look so happy. If you and your sheik have half the marriage Flynt and I do, then, you'll be happy for the rest of your life."

Cara returned the squeeze, then released Josie's hand. "There have been so many times in the past that guys have tried to get close to me just to be near Fiona. Or I've had an interest in a man, only to discover he's dated my sister and is still carrying a torch for her. If I tell Omar the truth too quickly, I'm afraid he'll walk away without a backward glance."

Josie's green eyes twinkled. "Are you trying to convince me or yourself?"

Cara grinned ruefully. "I'm not sure," she admitted. "Maybe both."

"Well, your secret is safe with me, but you'd better not wait too long to tell him. Sooner or later somebody in town or around here is going to call you Cara."

That was Cara's biggest fear. Over the past three days, thankfully, most of the time she had spent with Omar had been in his suite at the hotel, except for one evening when they had dinner with her parents.

Both Ford and Grace had abided by her wishes and had referred to her as Elizabeth throughout the evening. Ford had also made it clear to Omar that he expected his "little girl" to be allowed to fly home to visit whenever she wanted.

Omar had assured the Carson patriarch that he would never keep her away from the family she so obviously loved.

And in those three days, time and time again, Cara had tried to find the words to tell Omar the truth. But it seemed each time she got up the nerve to confess, something conspired to keep her silent. The phone would ring or a waiter would appear, and Cara would swallow her confession, vowing that she'd find a better place, a better time.

She now sat in the back of the limo that was carrying her from her cottage to Omar's hotel for lunch. She'd been surprised the driver had come to the door rather than Rashad.

In the past week she had come to like the little man with his wicked sense of humor and infectious smile. The trips to and from the hotel were made more enjoyable by Rashad's company.

And in the past three days her love for Omar had grown stronger. He was all she had ever dreamed of in a man. Each time he kissed her it grew more and more difficult to stand by her conviction to wait until their wedding night to make love with him. She hoped there would be a wedding night.

When they arrived at the hotel, Rashad was waiting for her just inside the lobby. "I regret that I was unable to accompany you today," he said as he walked with her to the elevator.

"Is everything all right?" she asked, noting the lines of tension that tightened his wizened features.

"Fine, fine," he said, but his taut smile told her otherwise. He handed her the key to reach the penthouse suite.

She rode alone in the elevator, but when the door opened into the suite, Omar wasn't there waiting for her. From the bedroom she could hear his voice. It was obvious he was on the phone, and the conversation was not pleasant.

"You tell them we are a small country, but we are not a stupid country." His voice held a power and authority she'd never heard before. "They are not negotiating, they are toying with us, and until they make a reasonable offer, I will no longer discuss anything with them."

Cara stood just inside the living room, uncomfortable over the fact that Omar wasn't aware of her presence. She heard him slam down the receiver, then pick it up once again.

"Rashad," he said. "Get me a copy of all of our trade agreements, particularly the ones dealing with Kyria, and bring it to me immediately."

Again she heard the crash of the receiver into the cradle, then he exited the bedroom. His mouth was a tight slash of fury and his eyes were darker than she'd ever seen them. His nostrils were flared, and the air around him seemed to pulsate with energy.

In that instant, Cara knew she was seeing Omar the Sheik. Power radiated from him, the powerful arrogance of a man accustomed to getting his way, the commanding assurance of a man who knew what he wanted and how to get it.

The moment he saw her, he visibly relaxed. "My dear," he said as he strode across the room and took her hand in his. "I apologize. I didn't hear you come in."

"I didn't want to interrupt you," she replied.

"You could only be a pleasant interruption." He led her to the sofa, where she sat while he remained standing. "As usual, you look positively gorgeous today."

"Thank you, but it sounds like you have more important things to attend to than lunch with me."

His eyes were gentle as he gazed at her. "And what could be more important than lunch with my fiancée?"

"Oil negotiations that will affect the future of your country," she replied. "We can have lunch together tomorrow, Omar, if now isn't a good time."

He smiled and leaned over to stroke a finger down her cheek. "Each day that we spend time together you do something to confirm how right I am to want you as my wife," he said softly. "And you just did it again."

The look in his eyes, the seductive quality of his voice and the heat of his caress made Cara feel as if she were melting inside. "I'm serious, Omar. If this is not a good time for you, we can arrange something for later."

"Unfortunately, there might not be a later," he replied. A soft bell indicated the arrival of the elevator.

The doors opened to reveal Rashad, a sheath of papers in his hand.

Omar took the papers from Rashad and clapped the small man on the back. "Thank you, Rashad. I'm sorry if I've been brusque with you this morning."

Rashad gave him a little bow, his dark eyes sparkling with impish humor. "I am at your disposal, Sheik Al Abdar, even when you have the mood of an ill-tempered camel."

Omar laughed, the deep, rich sound filling every chamber of Cara's heart. "I should have you beheaded for impudence," Omar said good-naturedly.

"Ah, but you would miss my impudence," Rashad replied with a toothy grin. With a bow, he turned and got back into the elevator.

"I like him," Cara said.

Omar joined her on the sofa and placed the papers on the coffee table before them. "He's impertinent and outspoken and can nag worse than an old woman, and I don't know what I would do without him."

"He mentioned that he worked for your father before working for you."

Omar nodded. "Rashad has been a trusted member of the Al Abdar family for as long as I can remember. But enough about him. I have more pressing matters on my mind. I fear our oil negotiations have completely broken down and I must return to Gaspar."

Thick disappointment overwhelmed her. "When?" she asked.

"I should leave immediately, but I would wait until

tomorrow if you would go with me as my wife." He reached out and took her hands in his. "Marry me, Elizabeth. Marry me this afternoon, right now, and go home with me tomorrow. I don't want to return to Gaspar without you at my side." He squeezed her hands, his eyes compelling her to acquiesce to his wishes.

Cara's heart thudded frantically in her chest as she felt herself falling into the beautiful depths of his eyes. *Tell him,* a tiny voice whispered in the back of her head. *Tell him now.*

"We can marry immediately and spend our wedding night here, then fly to Gaspar first thing tomorrow as husband and wife," he said. He pulled her into his arms, his mouth mere inches from hers. "Say yes, Elizabeth. Don't make me wait any longer to make you mine."

"Yes." The word hissed out of her on a sigh, and before she could fully accept what she'd just agreed to his lips were on hers, sweeping any doubts, any hesitation away with the mastery and force of the kiss.

When the kiss ended, she wasn't sure if she had just taken the first step into seeing her every dream come true, or just made the biggest mistake of her life.

The next hour went by in a blur. One minute Omar was kissing her in his penthouse suite, the next minute they were standing in a small lobby, awaiting the justice of the peace who was going to marry them.

Things were moving too fast, way too fast, and Cara didn't know how to slow them down. Her handsome sheik was sweeping her off her feet, and she was allowing him to do so.

"Omar, before we do this I really need to tell you something," she said with a touch of desperation.

At that moment Rashad burst through the door, his arms filled with a beautiful bouquet of flowers. "Ah, Rashad, I feared you wouldn't make it in time," Omar said as he took the bouquet from his assistant's arms.

He held the lovely flowers out to Cara. "I could not have my bride getting married to me without a proper bridal bouquet."

His voice was a warm, deep caress as he explained, "The violets stand for faithfulness, the daisies are for innocence, the lilies are for purity and, of course, the roses are for love."

Cara looked at him, awed by the obvious thought that had gone into the bouquet. Tears burned her eyes. "Omar, I'm afraid," she blurted out. "I'm not the woman you think I am."

The look he gave her was one of infinite tenderness, and he reached up and stroked the side of her cheek in a gesture that was becoming achingly familiar. "You are exactly the woman I think you are," he said. "Every moment I have spent with you has only made me more certain that you are the woman I want by my side."

At that moment Justice of the Peace Jerrold Walker motioned them into his office. Panic swelled inside Cara's chest, and she knew she should call a halt to everything.

But at that moment Omar took her hand in his. In his dark, beautiful eyes she saw the promise of the future she'd always dreamed of. And even though she knew she should tell him the truth, she didn't. She couldn't.

It was all wrong, but she hoped and prayed that it would eventually turn out all right.

It had all been wrong, Omar thought as he and Elizabeth were pronounced man and wife. He gathered her into his arms to kiss her and saw the tears that shimmered in her eyes.

"We will marry again in Gaspar," he said, believing he knew the reason for her tears. "And we will have your parents there, and your sister and brothers. It will be the wedding of your dreams, the wedding we didn't have time for today." He gave her no opportunity to reply, but instead claimed her mouth with his.

"That isn't necessary," she protested and with a small laugh of embarrassment she wiped away her tears. She was his now, bound to him through law and tradition. The woman who had bewitched him so long ago was now his bride, and the thought of possessing her completely filled him with a sweet rush of anticipation.

They left the justice of the peace and headed back to Omar's hotel. But as the car pulled up out front, she turned to him.

"Omar, I need to go home and speak with my parents. And I have to pack and prepare for the trip to

Gaspar." She appeared overwhelmed. She raked a hand through her dark brown wavy hair, and he noticed that her fingers shook slightly.

"Don't worry about packing too many things," he told her and smiled. "You will discover that I am a generous, indulgent husband, and whatever you need or want, you will receive."

"I still need to talk to my parents," she said. "I need to tell them what we've done before they hear it from anybody else.

He nodded. "Of course. We'll go directly to the ranch."

"I know it sounds silly, but I'd like to speak with them alone." Her gaze didn't quite meet his. "I would like some time to say goodbye."

He realized how difficult this would be for her. "Are you sure you'll be all right?" he asked gently, and she nodded. "Then, the car will take you there and the driver will wait until you are ready to return here."

He drew her small hand into his. "But don't take too long, my love." He raised her hand to his lips. "Because I can't wait to make love to you."

She laughed, a shaky, breathless sound that stirred him. "If you don't stop kissing my hand, we'll make love right here in the back of the limo—and that's not where I want to have my first experience." Her cheeks grew pink.

The reminder of her innocence shot a burst of desire through him. He would be a good lover with her, gentle and patient, and he would hold his passion in check until she was ready to be an equal partner in that arena.

Moments later, as the car pulled away from the curb, Omar and Rashad returned to Omar's suite, where Rashad began the task of packing and Omar stood at the window and stared out, thinking of the woman he'd just made his bride.

"You look troubled, Your Highness," Rashad observed.

Omar nodded. "I'm troubled about the negotiations and eager to return to Gaspar." He smiled at Rashad. "And I guess I'm a bit homesick. I'd like to counsel with my father and be back where I belong."

"Your father will be happy that you're returning a married man. I think he will approve of Elizabeth."

Omar's smile widened. "My father didn't care whom I married, just that I got married."

"He will consider it a bonus that you married a beautiful, intelligent, compassionate woman."

Omar raised an eyebrow. "Sounds like somebody has a crush on my wife." To his surprise, Rashad's face reddened.

"She is a nice lady," he replied.

"Yes, she is." Omar turned back to the window, a smile curving his lips as he thought of Elizabeth. She was different than he'd remembered her.

The woman he had met at the cotillion so long ago had seemed brazen, utterly fearless and a little bit spoiled. He was thankful that she had matured into a thoughtful, caring woman who would do him proud as his wife. He just hoped there was a touch of that brazen, adventurous woman still inside her. His blood heated as he thought of the night to come.

The phone rang, interrupting all thoughts of his wedding night. For the next two hours he was occupied with Gaspar business, taking first one phone call, then another.

"No more calls," he said to Rashad when he finally hung up. There were things he wanted to do to prepare the suite for tonight. But before he could call room service and order what he wanted, the phone rang once again.

"I said no more calls," he said, as Rashad held the receiver out to him.

"Beg your pardon, Your Highness, but I think you'll want to take this one," Rashad said. "It's your wife."

Omar took the phone. "Elizabeth, where are you, darling?"

"I just left the ranch, and my parents insisted they wanted to do something special for us for our wedding. I hope you don't mind, Omar, but they got us the bridal suite at the Lone Star Country Club for the night. I'm here now, and I sent the car back to you. I didn't know what to tell them, Omar," she said, obviously worried about his reaction.

"I hope you told them thank you," he replied.

"I did. And, Omar, I've ordered the champagne and I'll be waiting for you in the hot tub."

He grinned, his blood once again heating with anticipation. How could he have thought this woman was timid and not adventurous? "I'm on my way."

# Chapter 6

The bridal suite at the Lone Star Country Club was sumptuous. The living-room area held an elegant white sofa, the material shot through with gold-colored thread. The glass-top coffee table held an arrangement of fresh-cut flowers that filled the air with their perfume.

In one corner of the room was a wet bar, completely stocked, and in the opposite corner was a large sunken hot tub, the hot water spiraling steam upward.

Cara's parents had initially been upset that she and Omar had sneaked off to the justice of the peace and gotten married. But they had quickly offered her their love and support, as she knew they would, and her father had made the arrangements for them to have this suite for the night.

Because she had no idea what Omar's plans were for returning to Gaspar the next day, she had shared a tearful goodbye with her parents, with promises to write often and to return home for Christmas in six weeks.

As she had been packing a couple of suitcases, her mother had sat on the edge of her bed, talking to her about marriage and the responsibilities of a wife.

"You won't even be here for Thanksgiving," Grace exclaimed, her eyes filling with tears.

Cara sat on the edge of the bed next to her mother. "Mama, be happy that I'll be spending Thanksgiving in my new home with my new husband," she replied. "Be happy that I've found the man I want to spend the rest of my life with."

"I am happy for you, Cara." Her mother reached out and took Cara's hand in hers. "I just hope you didn't marry your sheik for the wrong reasons."

Cara looked at her mother curiously. "What do you mean?"

Grace smiled at her, a smile of such unconditional love that Cara felt it flowing through her. "You suffered quite a trauma at the end of last year with that student, and I hope that hasn't affected your judgment."

"It hasn't," Cara replied quickly, not wanting to think of those terrifying hours.

"You can't go through something like that and not have it change you," Grace observed.

"Still, that experience isn't what has made me jump into a marriage with Omar," Cara said firmly.

"Then, I hope you haven't married Omar in order to be in a new place with a new group of people, to escape your sister's presence." She held up a hand as Cara started to protest.

"I know you've always believed you live in Fiona's shadow, but the truth is, Cara, the only difference between you and your sister is that for some reason you lack Fiona's self-confidence. You are just as bright, just as beautiful and just as charming, but you've never really believed that."

Now, Cara shoved away thoughts of the conversation with her mother and went into the bedroom of the suite, where the sight of the king-size bed sent shivers of apprehension through her.

Tonight she and Omar would make love. Every nerve ending in her body tingled at the thought.

Omar would be here soon, and she had told him she'd be waiting for him in the hot tub. Her fingers trembled as she pulled her bathing suit from her suitcase.

If she was more like her sister, she'd be waiting in the hot tub naked, but she simply couldn't do that. She nearly jumped out of her skin when there was a knock on the door.

Surely it wasn't Omar already! She'd only just moments before called him to tell him she was here. She hurried to the door, opened it—and stared in shock at her sister.

"Fiona!" she exclaimed, and pulled her sister into the room. "What are you doing here?"

Fiona removed her oversize sunglasses. "I couldn't let you fly off tomorrow without saying goodbye." She wrapped her arms around Cara and gave her a hard hug. "I got home a little early—and apparently just in time. Mom and Dad told me what's going on—that you were here and would be leaving for Gaspar tomorrow."

Tears of joy burned in Cara's eyes. "I'm so glad you're here. I didn't want to leave without saying goodbye," she exclaimed.

"I can't believe you married him, Cara!" Fiona released her and stepped back. "I told you to have fun with this, to enjoy being engaged to a sheik. But I didn't expect you to marry him."

"I didn't expect to marry him, either," Cara replied. "But I love him, Fiona, and I'm sure he loves me."

"So, how did he take it when you told him the truth about you writing the letters instead of me?" Fiona asked.

Cara averted her gaze from her twin. "Oh my God, Cara, you haven't told him the truth?"

"I've tried," Cara exclaimed fervently. "I've tried several times, but the timing was never right, or something happened and I lost my nerve."

Fiona's eyes sparkled with amusement. "My devious sister, I never would have thought it of you." Then the light in her eyes dimmed. "Oh God, Cara, I'm going to miss you terribly."

This time it was Cara who reached for her sister, and again they hugged. "I'm going to miss you, too," Cara said. "But I love him, Fiona, and I want to spend my life with him."

"Let me see the ring." Fiona grasped Cara's left hand and squealed at the sight of the lovely emerald. "Maybe I made a big mistake in not continuing to write him," she teased. "And I guess I'd better get out of here before he shows up." She stepped away from Cara. "You'll call me often?"

"You know I will," Cara replied, her heart aching as she realized the path she'd chosen to follow was truly taking her away from her family and everything she'd known all her life.

Fiona opened the door to leave, then turned back to Cara with a smile. "If you really love him, and he loves you, then I envy you, Cara. I've always envied you, but now more than ever." She leaned forward and kissed Cara's cheek. "Be happy," she said, then before Cara could reply, she turned and hurried down the hallway.

Cara closed the door, tears once again stinging her eyes. She was going to miss her twin sister desperately. She was going to miss her parents, and her little cottage and her brothers and their wives.

She was going to miss it all, but it was time to put her past behind her and embrace her future. Her future with Omar.

She returned to the bathroom and once again

grabbed her swimsuit. As she changed into the demure one-piece, her mother's words haunted her.

Had she married Omar for all the wrong reasons? Had it been a combination of wanting to escape Fiona's bright light and some sort of delayed reaction to being held at gunpoint by a distraught student?

And what had Fiona meant by telling her that she'd always been envious of her? Why on earth would Fiona have any reason to envy Cara? She dismissed the very idea from her mind. Then she thought of Fiona calling her "devious."

She wasn't devious. She hadn't set out to deceive Omar. It had all just spun out of control.

When the brief marriage ceremony had ended, she'd held her breath when the justice of the peace gave Omar a copy of the marriage license. To her immense relief, Omar had instantly handed it to Rashad, without looking at the signature.

Omar might believe he'd married Elizabeth Fiona Carson, but on the marriage certificate she'd signed Elizabeth C. Carson, she thought as she pinned her hair up on top of her head.

She stared at her reflection in the mirror. She'd married Omar under false pretenses and she truly didn't know if she'd married him for all the wrong reasons. She only knew she wanted to stay married to him for all the *right* reasons.

She left the bathroom and walked back into the living room. The champagne was on ice, and a tray of fresh fruit, cheese and crackers awaited their nibbling pleasure.

She thought of pouring herself a glass of champagne to ease some of the nervous tension that flowed through her, but dismissed the idea and instead slid into the hot tub.

The hot water instantly soothed her tight muscles, wrapping around her like a soothing massage. She leaned her head back and closed her eyes, thinking of Omar.

He had mistaken her tears immediately after the marriage ceremony, believing that she was mourning the fairy-tale wedding she wasn't getting.

His response to her that he would see to it she had a dream wedding once they got settled in Gaspar had only made her feel worse about her deception.

One thing was certain, she vowed to be the wife he deserved. More than anything, she never wanted to give him a reason to think that he'd married the wrong sister.

She opened her eyes, tension peaking as she heard the sound of a key in the door.

Omar entered, closed the door behind him, then stood, his dark eyes blazing with passion. "What a vision you are," he exclaimed, his voice low, husky and flowing over her as sensually as the water that surrounded her.

"Why don't you pour us a glass of champagne and join me?" It was the most brazen thing she'd ever said to a man, but she reminded herself that this wasn't just any man. This was her husband, the man with whom she intended to spend the rest of her life.

He dropped the small overnight bag he carried. "That sounds like a marvelous idea." He took off his suit jacket and draped it over the back of the sofa. Then, his gaze still locked with hers, he began unbuttoning his shirt.

Cara's heart beat with a delicious rhythm as his broad, firmly muscled chest was revealed.

During the last week of his visit, they had indulged in heated kisses, and shared intimate meals and conversations, but she hadn't seen him when he wasn't impeccably and properly dressed.

The shirt fell to the floor, and her mouth grew dry as he kicked off his shoes, then unzipped his pants. The water around her seemed to get hotter as his pants slid from his slender hips onto the floor, leaving him clad only in a pair of socks and black silk boxer shorts.

He was absolutely gorgeous. As he bent over to remove his socks, she drank in the beauty of his physical appearance. Not only was his chest muscled, but his stomach was lean, without an ounce of body fat. His hips were slim, but his legs were powerfully built.

Omar was a poster boy for physical fitness, and Cara couldn't believe he was really her husband. Nor could she fathom that within minutes he would possess her completely. She shivered despite the heat of the water.

After several days or weeks of marriage, after they

had made love a dozen times or so, then she would tell him the truth about her identity. Surely by then it wouldn't matter to him. He would realize she was the woman he loved.

"There's cheese and crackers and fruit if you want any," she said as she watched him pour the champagne into two fluted glasses. "I didn't order any dinner yet. I wasn't sure what you would want."

"We can eat later," he said as he walked toward the hot tub. He held one of the glasses out to her, then eased down into the water and sat next to her.

His shoulder pressed against hers, as did his hip and thigh, and as he took a sip of his champagne he put an arm around her, pulling her even closer against his side. She tensed, unsure what to expect, afraid and excited of what was to come.

Cara took a deep swallow of the chilled champagne, as his fingers caressed her arm.

"Relax, my sweet," he said softly. "I promise I don't intend to ravish you in the next few minutes."

She smiled up at him. "I have to admit, I'm a bit nervous."

"There's nothing to be nervous about." His gaze was tender. "I promise I'll do everything in my power to make tonight the most wonderful night of your life."

With the sweet heat flowing from his eyes and the promise on his lips, her tension dissipated. There was no reason to be nervous, she told herself.

This man was her husband, and she loved him. Making love to him would only complete the union that had begun the moment they said their vows to each other.

"This feels wonderful," he said, and smiled at her. "A perfect way to unwind from the day. Were your parents angry with us?"

"Not angry, but definitely upset. I explained to them that things happened very fast, that you have to return to Gaspar in the morning and I wanted to go with you as your wife. I also reminded them that you have said I can return home for visits often."

He nodded. "As often as you like. I would never do anything to keep you from your family." He took a sip of his champagne, then set the glass on the tiled edge around the tub. He scooted deeper into the water, his leg rubbing sensually against hers, then reached out and took her glass from her.

Cara's heart seemed to stop beating for a moment. He placed her glass next to his, then gathered her into his arms. The water made her body buoyant, as he pulled her between his outstretched legs. He held her more tightly against him, and she felt the evidence of his arousal. Her heart renewed its frantic beating.

"You look pretty with your hair up," he said, his lips mere inches from hers. His hands moved up and down her back, electrifying her through the thin material of her bathing suit.

"I feel as if I've been waiting for this night, for you, for a very long time."

Cara wondered if he was thinking of the young woman he'd flirted with at the cotillion so long ago or the woman whose letters had touched his heart.

It didn't matter, for at that moment his lips met hers, and she was overwhelmed with the taste of him, the mastery of his kiss and the sensations of his hands stroking her back.

His mouth ravished hers, his tongue swirling with hers in erotic play. The sensations that flooded her were intoxicating. The hot water surrounding them, the feel of his powerful arousal against her, and the hot wonder of his mouth against hers—all combined to create in her a desire she'd never experienced before.

When his lips left hers, they blazed a trail down the side of her neck, nibbled lightly on her earlobe, then moved down across her collarbone.

Cara tightened her grip on his shoulders, gasping with pleasure at each touch of his lips.

"You are so beautiful," he whispered against her ear.

He placed one arm beneath her legs and the other around her back, and in one smooth movement stood with her in his arms. "I think it's time to move out of the hot tub," he said. "Don't you?"

She nodded, as he stood her on her feet next to the tub and grabbed one of the thick white towels that awaited nearby. He began drying her, rubbing the towel briskly over her shoulders.

As he moved the towel down the length of her, he rubbed less briskly and more slowly, sensually, until she didn't feel she was being dried, but rather caressed.

He lingered over her breasts, his eyes holding hers as he gently stroked the towel across her. Her knees weakened as he dried her tummy, then swept the towel first down one leg, then the other.

He threw the towel to the side and started to pick her up once again.

"Not so fast," she murmured, and reached over to pick up a fresh towel.

She moved to stand behind him and rubbed the towel across the muscled expanse of his naked back. She saw his muscles flex, felt the energy that radiated from him, and thrilled that it was her touch making him so tightly drawn.

As she stroked the towel across his firm buttocks, he tensed even more and his breathing became more rapid, matching her own. She had never touched a man so intimately, and she found the experience unbelievably thrilling. She had never known her touch had the ability to turn on a man, but it was obvious that was exactly what she was doing to Omar.

She moved to stand in front of him and swiped the towel across his broad chest, then leaned forward and pressed her lips against the place where she knew his heart was beating as frantically as her own.

With a groan of pleasure, he pulled the towel from

her hands and tossed it to the floor. "I think perhaps we should change and have a bite to eat."

His voice was almost guttural, and his eyes glittered with a passion that nearly stole her breath away.

He smiled and touched her lips with the tip of his finger. "If we continue like this, we will be finished almost before we begin. I don't want the first time we make love to be fast and frantic." He removed his finger from her lips. "Why don't you get into something dry, and I'll do the same."

She nodded, still in a half haze from the desire that welled inside her. She turned and went into the bedroom, where her overnight bag was open on the edge of the bed. She grabbed a pair of lacy panties and the dress box that was next to her suitcase, then went into the bathroom.

The box contained a gorgeous white peignoir set. It had been delivered fifteen minutes after she checked into the room—a gift from her mother.

Her fingers trembled as she changed out of her bathing suit and into the lace-trimmed silk nightgown and matching robe.

As she stared at her reflection in the bathroom mirror, she was suddenly struck by how quickly everything had transpired. She had known Omar for less than a week, and now she was married to him.

She was flying off to a country she'd never visited, with a man she hardly knew, to live with him as his wife.

And all of it was based on a lie.

* * *

Omar changed from his soaking wet boxers to a silk robe, and moved the food tray and champagne into the bedroom. The room was dark, with heavy curtains blocking out the last of the day's light. He turned on the bedside lamp, which cast a soft, golden glow around the room.

He couldn't remember the last time he'd been so inflamed by a woman, and he knew much of Elizabeth's appeal was her charming combination of innocence and natural seductiveness.

As he pulled the bedspread from the bed and stretched out on the pristine sheets, he congratulated himself on his choice of a wife.

His father would be pleased. Elizabeth was beautiful and intelligent, and would be a support to Omar as he ruled his kingdom. She came from a good family background, and she would be a gracious hostess to visiting dignitaries in Gaspar.

He had made his decision to marry her without the heat of passion, guided solely on the basis of a single memory of meeting her and the letters they had exchanged. It was an added bonus that he desired her.

They would have a good marriage, and she would never have to know that love didn't enter into it. Omar had learned from the wisest man he knew that love made a man weak, that a leader's heart belonged only to his country, not to any woman. That man had been Omar's father, the man Omar respected more than anyone on earth.

All thoughts of his father disappeared as the bathroom door opened and she stood there for a moment, absolutely stunning in a white silk nightgown and matching robe. Her hair was still pinned atop her head, with tendrils escaping the pins to frame her lovely face.

"Come join me," he said, and patted the bed next to him. He could see her nervousness in the stiff way she walked across the room and in the slight tremble of her lower lip as she stretched out on the bed next to him.

He sat up and poured them both a fresh glass of champagne, then held his glass out to hers. "To us," he said. "May we grow old together and raise our children to be strong and good." He smiled. "And may our desire for each other only grow stronger with each year that passes."

He clinked his glass to hers, and they both sipped the chilled bubbly. "You look as if you're about to face the executioner," he observed.

She smiled, the gesture drawing his attention to the beauty mark that danced just above her lips on the left side of her face.

"I can't help it that I'm nervous. I've never had a wedding night before."

"Neither have I," he replied.

Her long-lashed green eyes held his gaze. "And I've never made love with a man before."

"Neither have I."

She laughed, and a sweet warmth flooded through

him at the melodious sound. "You know what I'm talking about," she said more soberly. "I'm sure you've had many lovers."

"I've had lovers," he agreed. "I'm thirty-eight years old, Elizabeth. It's true, I have not lived my life as a monk." He reached out a hand and drew his fingers down the soft curve of her cheek. "But that's all in my past. Now there's only one woman in my life—you."

Her cheeks blushed with a charming pink hue. "And there's only one man in my life, and that's you," she said.

Suddenly Omar wanted to wait no longer. His thought had been to eat some of the tidbits, drink some champagne and talk until she was completely at ease. But he was not hungry for bits of cheese and fruit. He was hungry for her.

He watched as she sipped her champagne, his desire increasing as her pink tongue slid across her lower lip. He downed the last of his champagne in one quick swallow, then took her glass from her and set it on the nightstand.

He turned back to her and gathered her into his arms. She came willingly, as if eager to accept his lessons in lovemaking.

As he kissed her, her mouth opened eagerly beneath his and he felt his control slipping. She smelled of sweet spring flowers, and her body radiated a warmth he wanted to explore.

His hands slid up and down the silky material on

her back, and the kiss lingered until she was half breathless and so was he.

He moved his hands to the front, where her robe was fastened with tiny seed buttons. His fingers fumbled, clumsy with anticipation. Finally he got the robe unfastened, and she sat up to help him remove it.

Beneath the robe, the white silk nightgown left little to his imagination. The spaghetti straps exposed her creamy shoulders, and the deep, plunging neckline revealed the lush curves of her breasts.

"You are so beautiful," he said, and felt himself swelling with intense desire for her. He flicked one of the spaghetti straps from her shoulder and pressed his lips against her smooth, satiny skin.

Her flesh was hot, as if fevered by an internal flame. As he loved her shoulder with his mouth and his tongue, she emitted a tiny moan of pleasure that stirred him to the depths of his soul.

He ran one hand down her side, along her rib cage and over her hip, then back again. As his mouth sought hers once again, he captured a breast with his hand, able to feel her turgid nipple through the silk material.

She gasped against his mouth as his thumb raked over the peak, teasing and toying in sensual play. He wanted to stroke her sweet skin until she was mindless, wanted to kiss her until her head was filled with nothing but thoughts of him and her body ached with the need for fulfillment.

Although he was ravenous for her, he didn't want

to hurry. He wanted to savor every moment, each sensation, knowing that this night would be branded forever in his memory, but even more so in hers.

She would only have her initiation into lovemaking once, and he wanted to make certain that she never regretted that she'd chosen him to share the experience.

He slid his hand beneath the silk and cupped her breast in his hand as his mouth left hers and followed the path of his hand. The barrier of the nightgown frustrated him.

He raised his head and looked at her, noting with satisfaction that her eyes were hooded and glazed with passion. "I want you naked," he whispered.

Using one hand, he pulled her gown up to midthigh. She raised her hips, allowing him to pull the material up farther, exposing a delicate pair of lacy panties.

He swept the nightgown up and over her head and tossed it to the floor, then he removed his robe, leaving him naked and fully aroused.

He pulled her back into his arms, pressing his nakedness fully against her length. "There is nothing more exciting than the touch of skin against skin," he murmured. "And it's amazing how many erogenous places there are on the human body." His lips trailed up the column of her slender neck and lingered at the spot just behind her ear. "Like just behind the ear…"

He moved his lips from there down to the hollow of her throat. "And here." She shivered and grabbed his shoulders.

Her fingers bit into his shoulders, as his mouth

moved to capture the tip of her breast. He'd thought
he'd be a teacher and slowly educate her in the many
ways of pleasure, but as she arched against him, pressing herself intimately against his arousal, he felt his
control slipping, as if he were caught in a tidal wave
of desire too intense to fight.

*Chapter 7*

Cara had never felt so incredibly liquid, as if it weren't simply blood that flowed through her veins, but rather heated honey. Each kiss Omar gave her increased the tension that created an ache deep within the pit of her stomach.

His mouth loved her skin, leaving every inch kissed or caressed. His body was hot against hers, hot and hard, and as he explored her, she did the same to him, running her hands across the muscular width of his back, stroking her fingers across his chest, caressing the length of his thigh.

She reveled in his response, loving the sound of his deep, throaty moans and the tension that she could feel seize him at her merest touch.

She had never before felt so wonderfully feminine,

as if she had been specially made to receive the love of a man. And Omar was the man who sang through her veins, resounded in her heartbeat, shot fire through her entire body.

When he slid her panties from her, she was ready for that intimacy, lost in a sensual haze that demanded something more than what he'd given her so far.

His fingers lightly stroked her where no man had ever touched her before, and the ache in her stomach intensified to mammoth proportions. It was both a little frightening and more than a little exciting.

As he increased the pressure of his touch, she felt herself climbing to heights of pleasure she'd never known before. Frightening heights, wondrous heights.

She knew she would die if he stopped touching her, but feared she might die if he continued. Then she felt herself shattering as wave after wave of the most intense pleasure she'd ever known swept through her, leaving her limp and exhausted.

He gave her no opportunity to recover from the magnificent sensations that overwhelmed her, but immediately moved his body between her thighs and entered her.

He slid into her, but halted as she stiffened, anticipating pain. "Are you all right?" he asked, his voice deep with tension, yet filled with warmth and concern.

She nodded and pulled him deeper into her. Although there was a moment of discomfort, it quickly gave way to pleasure.

He remained unmoving, buried in her and she could feel his heart beating a frantic rhythm against her own. His dark eyes bore into hers, communicating silently his own rampant desire.

She felt herself falling into his beautiful eyes, burned by the fires that sizzled there. Shudders racked her body, shudders of sweet sensation.

It was she who moved first, arching her hips into his, then pulling back in an action that was both primal and instinctive.

His eyes narrowed and a sigh escaped his lips. Then he was moving, driving into her as his mouth ravished hers. She felt as if her heart was going to burst out of her chest, so overwhelmed was she by the unfamiliar physical and emotional sensations.

Faster and faster they moved together, and a wild, gripping tension once again welled up inside her, a tension she knew only he could release.

She cried out in a combination of pleasure and need, and he increased the frenzied coupling, his breath coming in frantic gasps to match her own.

She cried out his name as she felt herself splintering apart. She clung to him as he stiffened, the cords in his neck strained. He moaned her name over and over again, his voice deep and husky, and a moment later relaxed and rolled to the side of her.

For several minutes the only sound in the room was that of the two of them trying to catch their breath. When Cara finally felt more in control, she reached with her hand to find the sheet to cover herself, but Omar stopped her.

"Don't hide yet," he said. He propped himself up on his elbow and smiled. "Part of the pleasure of love-making is the visual treat of seeing your beauty."

As his eyes traveled slowly down the length of her, lingering first at her breasts, then sweeping slowly down the rest of her, she felt his gaze as hot, as intimate as if he were trailing his hands over her.

"You are so beautiful," he murmured.

His gaze once again held hers, this time lit with concern, and he gently brushed a strand of her hair away from her cheek. "Did I hurt you?"

"Not at all." She felt her cheeks warm. "In fact, it was wonderful."

One of his dark eyebrows danced up and his eyes sparkled with a teasing light. "Only wonderful? Not magnificent? Not unbelievable? Not stupendous?" He gave her a mock frown. "I guess I will have to work harder next time."

She laughed, but her heart quickened at the thought of next time.

Omar gathered her into his arms, and she loved the way their naked skin felt pressed together. "I had thought to take it slow, to ease you into the joys of lovemaking, but you made it impossible for me to take it slow," he said.

He stroked his hand up her outer thigh, sending currents of electricity through her. "You are more passionate, more responsive and exciting than I had dreamed."

He leaned down and touched her lips with his in a soft, sweet kiss that warmed her heart. "Are you hungry? We never got around to supper."

"No." She snuggled closer to him, feeling safe and suddenly drowsy. "I'm perfectly content right here."

She pressed her face against his chest, loving the scent of him, a clean male scent with just a hint of spicy cologne.

As sleep closed in, her last conscious thought was that surely Omar wouldn't be too angry when he learned the truth—not after what they'd just shared. Surely when the time came, he would be able to forgive her for her deception.

Luke Callaghan hacked his way through a thick growth of vines and cursed the name El Jefe. El Jefe was the terrorist group that had brought Luke to this godforsaken jungle.

He paused to swipe sweat from his eyes with the back of his arm. All around him, men were working to forge through the thicket of wrist-size vines that impeded their forward progress.

It was a hellish task, in sweltering heat that sapped all energy. He and the other men were beyond exhaustion. Riddled with insect bites, chafed from the relentless humidity, but driven to succeed in their mission for freedom, the men pushed forward.

The *rat-tat-tat* of machine-gun fire sent Luke and

his men to the soggy, swampy ground. Dammit. Intelligence had led them to believe that the rebels were several miles ahead of them.

Another burst of gunfire spat through the trees, and one of the men to Luke's left groaned and grabbed his thigh, where blood quickly covered his pants and hand.

"Sir, the fire seems to be coming from over there." One of the men pointed to a small rise on their right. "I think we can take them if a couple of us go circle around and get behind them."

"Take three men and go," Luke said, then slid along the ground toward the wounded man. "Stevens, you all right?"

The soldier nodded, although his youthful face was pale and a thick sheen of sweat clung to his forehead. Luke pushed his hand away and looked at the wound. "Doesn't seem to have hit an artery, but we need to get you out of here and back to the medics."

At that moment another burst of gunfire hit, snapping bark off trees and pumping into the ground around them. He looked back at Stevens. "We aren't going anywhere at the moment."

Stevens nodded, knowing they were pinned down by the enemy fire.

Luke swept his gaze around the area, making certain none of the other men had been hurt or killed. He'd seen far too much death already on this mission.

Moments ticked by, then an explosion ripped through the air, coming from the direction where the gunfire had originated. Luke prayed that the explosion was the result of his men taking out the nest of terrorists. But he could take nothing for granted.

He had a bad feeling in his gut about this entire mission. Nothing was going smoothly, and he feared things were going to get worse before they got better.

He sighed in relief as word came that it was safe for them to continue on. As medics rushed forward to attend to the wounded, Luke pulled himself up off the ground, wondering when their luck was going to run out.

The bad feeling in the pit of his stomach hadn't gone away. It had only intensified.

Gunshots spat from the gun Donny Albright held in his hand, and Cara felt the bullets piercing her body. She cried out in terror and pain, trying to run, trying to escape the assault.

"Shh, it's just a dream." A deep, male voice cut through horrible images, soothing her as strong arms wrapped around her. "You're safe, darling. You're here, safe with me."

Cara came awake long enough to realize she'd been suffering a nightmare. As Omar pulled her closer against his warm, snuggly form, whispering words of assurance, she relaxed and drifted back into a dreamless, peaceful sleep.

When she awakened again, the room was still black but she was alone in the bed. She heard the sound of water running in the bathroom and realized it must be early morning—Omar was in the shower.

Omar her husband. Omar her lover. She stretched languidly and placed a hand on the pillow that still held the indentation of his head. And what a lover he had been.

A delicious feeling swept through her as she thought of the lovemaking they had shared. She'd always known that making love could be beautiful and special, but nothing had prepared her for the utter wonder of it all.

Omar had been so gentle, yet so masterful. He'd made her introduction into the world of physical pleasure truly magical.

As she remembered how sweetly he'd comforted her after her nightmare, her heart expanded with love for the man she had married.

She sat up and looked at the clock on the nightstand. Just after six. She slid out of the bed, grabbed her robe from the floor and pulled it on around her, then went to the windows and opened the curtains.

The morning sun was just peeking over the horizon, a glorious sunrise in brilliant reds and oranges. Her breath caught in her chest at the beauty. She felt as if the sunrise had been sent just to her, a promise of her future with Omar.

She was just about to turn away from the window, when firm male arms wrapped around her from behind. "Good morning," his deep voice breathed into her ear.

She leaned back against him, loving the way his body felt so solid and surprisingly familiar. His freshly showered scent filled her senses. "Good morning," she replied. "I was just admiring the beautiful sunrise."

"I'm glad you like it. I ordered it special, just for you," he said.

"Ah, you are a good and thoughtful husband," she said, and turned to face him.

He smiled and ran his hands up and down her back. "I would much rather feast my eyes on you than a mere sunrise."

"I have married not only a magnificent lover but a charmer, as well."

He laughed and lightly touched the tip of her nose with his index finger. "Why don't you go take a shower, and I'll order some coffee. I told Rashad we'd meet him at the airstrip around seven."

"Then, I'd better get showered and dressed," she said. As Omar picked up the phone to order coffee, she grabbed her clothes from her suitcase and went into the bathroom.

She was almost reluctant to shower; her skin still retained the scent of him. But she reminded herself that what they'd shared the night before was only the beginning. There would be many, many nights of Omar making love to her.

Moments later she stood beneath the hot spray of water, excitement beginning to build inside her as she thought of traveling to Gaspar.

Her new country. Her new home. Omar's descriptions of the little country had been colorful and vivid, and she was already half in love with her new homeland.

She gasped in surprise as the glass door to the shower opened and a splendidly naked Omar stepped inside. "I don't believe I had an opportunity to complete your education of erogenous zones last night," he said, and took the bar of soap from her fingers.

"What about the coffee?" she asked, her heartbeat racing as he stroked the soap across her shoulders.

"We can have coffee on the jet," he said, his gaze hot and hungry and creating an ache inside her.

"But won't we be late to meet Rashad?" The question escaped her on a moan of pleasure, as he lathered her breasts, then slid one of his hands down her stomach.

"Rashad will not mind waiting. He would approve of our reason for being late," he murmured, his lips flames of fire along the side of her throat.

As he pulled her beneath the warm water, his hands and lips creating magic, she forgot all about coffee, Rashad and an awaiting jet plane.

Omar's private jet had all the amenities of a top-notch hotel, and pride filled him as he escorted his new bride aboard. He introduced her to his pilot and the crew, then led her into the first compartment, which served as an office.

A beautiful teakwood desk held all the latest technology that Omar would need to command his country from the air. There was also a small conference table with several captain chairs covered with a beige, butter-soft leather.

Omar led his wife into the compartment beyond, which was outfitted like a living room and done in the official Gaspar colors of white, deep purple and gold.

"Omar, it's beautiful," she exclaimed as she sat on the white sofa and ran a hand over the purple throw pillows with gold trim.

"I prefer not to spend a lot of time flying, but when I must, I enjoy being comfortable," he said as he sat next to her. "There is a complete bath through that door." He pointed to a doorway. "And beyond that is a gourmet kitchen and a chef awaiting our dining pleasure."

"Very impressive," she said.

"I'll tell you what I find very impressive," he said. "You." His blood warmed as he thought of the lovemaking they had shared less than an hour before. "We must make it a practice to shower together as often as possible."

She smiled and blushed charmingly. "I've never had my back scrubbed so thoroughly," she replied.

He took her hand in his and drew it to his lips. "And I've never enjoyed scrubbing a back so thoroughly." He released her hand and grew more serious. "It's a long flight to Gaspar and I'm afraid there is business I must attend to during the flight."

"Don't worry about me," she said quickly. "I'll be just fine right here."

"There is reading material, or you are welcome to watch a movie," he said as he released her hand. "I'll be in the office next door, should you require anything."

"I'll be fine, really," she assured him.

A few minutes later, as the jet engines wound up for takeoff, he sank into his desk chair and thought again of what a good choice he'd made in Elizabeth.

He was grateful that she seemed to understand the demands on his time, that she didn't appear to be the kind of woman who would be jealous of the hours he needed to work at running his country.

What was interesting to him was that when he was with her, she somehow managed to make him forget that he was a sheik. She treated him like a man, looked at him as a man, and it was a refreshing difference from the way he'd been treated all his life.

He was eager to get her to Gaspar, to share the beauty and wonder of his country with her. There was a childlike quality to her, an innocence that he found delightful. In showing her the beauty of Gaspar, he would rediscover his country through her eyes.

Rashad entered the office, a smile lighting his diminutive features. "It will be good to get home," he said as he sat in one of the chairs at the conference table.

"Yes," Omar agreed. "I enjoy visiting the States,

but I'm ready to get home and get back to the business of Gaspar."

For the next two hours, that was exactly what Omar did—took care of business. Phone calls were made to his key advisors, letting them know his approximate time of arrival. He received updates on the oil negotiations and other trade agreements and on domestic situations that needed his attention.

He returned to the compartment with Elizabeth when it was time for lunch. He found her thumbing through a magazine, and her eyes lit with pleasure as he walked in.

"I thought you might be getting hungry," he said as he sat next to her on the sofa.

"I wasn't until I started smelling wonderful scents coming from the kitchen."

Omar smiled. "The chef has just let me know that our lunch is ready." He pointed to the table on the opposite side of the compartment. "Will you join me for lunch, my wife?"

She smiled prettily. "I would be delighted."

They moved to the table, and within minutes were being served a delicious meal of chicken cordon bleu and fresh steamed vegetables.

"It will be after midnight in Gaspar when we land, and I've told my staff there is nothing we will need for the night. Tomorrow morning we will breakfast with my father in his quarters." He saw the edge of nervousness that shadowed her eyes and smiled. "And my father will find you as charming, as beautiful and as perfect as I do."

She laughed. "I think I've married a sweet-talking man," she said, her green eyes sparkling with the teasing light he found so intoxicating.

"I intend to sweet-talk you every day of your life," he said.

For a moment her eyes were somber, and she held his gaze intently. "I hope so," she said, and her intensity surprised him.

He wondered if she was having doubts. "Elizabeth, I know you're leaving behind all you know and love to be my wife. I promise you that I will spend every day of my life making sure that you are never sorry for the choice you made," he said.

To his surprise, her eyes grew misty with tears. "And I hope, Omar, that you are never, ever sorry that I'm the person you married," she replied.

"I can't imagine that ever happening," he said as he reached across the table and took one of her hands in his.

He was touched by her obvious sentimentality, something he hadn't really expected from the kind of woman he'd thought her to be.

"And now let's talk about what some of your duties will be as my wife," he said, wanting to erase the tears from her eyes.

He explained to her that her main duty as his wife would be to present herself with dignity and grace, and function as hostess and helpmate at a variety of functions. "But of course your number-one priority is keeping me happy," he said with a grin.

She raised one of her eyebrows. "That sounds a bit chauvinistic."

He laughed. "It's only chauvinistic if I don't intend to make keeping you happy one of *my* priorities," he replied easily.

She smiled, her eyes clear and shining. "I am happy."

"I hope you say the same thing a year from now."

Again her eyes held an intensity that seemed out of proportion to the topic of the conversation. "And I hope you're happy with me a year from now."

After lunch, when Omar was once again seated at his desk, he thought of Elizabeth's unusual seriousness and was again struck by how emotional women could be. Women worried far too much about love and forever and such nonsense.

They had been married less than twenty-four hours, and it seemed she was already worried about the future of their marriage.

Of course their marriage would work. He'd chosen to marry Elizabeth after much thought on the subject.

Their marriage would work because *failure* was not a word in Omar's vocabulary.

The rest of the flight was uneventful. Omar divided his time between the two compartments, working for a while, then visiting with his wife. They shared an evening meal together, then Omar returned to his office to complete the last of the work he could accomplish while in the air.

It was just after midnight local time when the jet landed at the airstrip on the palace grounds. An official car awaited them, and moments after landing they were being driven to the palace.

He heard Elizabeth's gasp as his home came into view, and pride filled him. To say that Gaspar Palace was impressive was an understatement. Although more than a dozen buildings officially made up the compound that was the palace, the main building rose upward, pink marble and granite capped by a dome that seemed to attempt to meet the moon.

Several other, smaller domes topped other areas of the main building, giving the illusion of a Taj Mahal-type structure.

Although it was magnificent to behold, for Omar it was simply home, and his heart filled with the sweet comfort of returning to the place of his birth, the place where his children would be born.

He saw the awe on Elizabeth's face as they drew closer. "Oh, Omar, it's beautiful," she exclaimed, and reached for his hand.

He gave her hand a squeeze. "Welcome to your new home."

# Chapter 8

For the first time since she'd said "I do" to Omar, the enormity of being a sheik's wife struck her as she viewed her new home.

She'd been awed when she'd gotten her first glimpse of the palace, and the feeling continued as she and Omar entered the huge doors that led into a foyer the size of Cara's cottage in Texas.

The ceiling was covered with decorative ceramic tiles and inlaid with opals, jade and amethysts. The marble walls were covered with the official flag of Gaspar and silk tapestries in the royal colors. Beneath their feet, the floor was covered with luxurious oriental carpets.

"I will give you the full tour in the morning," Omar

said as he led her toward a huge staircase. "For tonight, we'll just go to our private quarters."

She nodded, too overwhelmed by it all to reply. The place was cavernous, with passageways and corridors leading in every direction. "I'll need to leave bread crumbs on the floor to find my way," she murmured.

Omar laughed and squeezed her arm as they ascended the stairs. "It won't take you long to learn the layout. Just remember, when you reach the top of the main stairway, our personal quarters are on the right. My father lives in the left wing."

They reached the top of the stairs and went down another hallway, then approached a large double door where uniformed guards stood on either side.

"Good evening, sir," one of the two said. "And welcome home."

"Thank you, Abba. It is good to be home," Omar replied. "And may I present my new bride, Elizabeth."

Both the guards bowed to Cara, then Abba opened the door between them. Cara gasped as Omar grabbed her and swung her up into his arms. "The West has some charming traditions, and one of them is carrying the bride over the threshold," he said as he stepped into the haven that was his private dwelling.

Before she could get a glimpse of her immediate surroundings, he kissed her gently on the lips. "I'm so glad you're here with me."

"I'm glad, as well," she replied, then gasped as he set her down inside and closed the door behind them. "It's all so beautiful," she exclaimed.

They stood in a large living area that radiated warmth and comfort. Two sofas faced each other, their beige material covered with colorful throw pillows. One entire wall appeared to be a state-of-the-art theater system complete with big-screen television and a stereo system that looked as if it would do everything except clean house.

"This is where I'm able to shed my responsibilities and worries as leader of my country and simply enjoy some quiet time as a man," he said.

She pointed to the theater system. "That doesn't look exactly conducive to quiet time," she teased.

"I confess, I'm a sucker for good movies." His dark eyes glittered brightly, sending a sweet heat rushing through her. "But I think my evenings will be better occupied now." There was a promise in his words, in the flames of his eyes, and a shiver of anticipation fluttered up her spine.

He led her from the living room into a formal dining room exquisitely decorated and big enough to seat twelve to fifteen people. Beyond that was a small breakfast nook with a breathtaking view of formal gardens, and beyond that the sparkling blue sea.

Within minutes of the brief tour, her head was spinning. In addition to a library and study and sunroom, there were also half a dozen gorgeous guest rooms and baths.

As he led her from room to room, he explained about the maids and secretaries, the cooks and other staff she would meet in the morning.

Still, nothing she'd seen so far had prepared her for the utter splendor and magnificence of the master bedroom. It looked like something from a version of *Arabian Nights*.

The bed was bigger than a king-size and covered with a luxurious deep purple spread. Shimmering silk in vivid purples, reds and turquoises cascaded down from the ceiling, falling on all sides of the bed to produce a gauzy, romantic enclosure.

Huge pillows were scattered about the room, providing places perfect to curl up with a book or merely stretch out to daydream. Floor-to-ceiling windows and a French door along one wall provided a view of what Omar said was a private little garden and the sea.

The master bath was just as impressive, with a sunken bathtub big enough to swim in and a shower and sauna nearby. Decorative jars of bath salts and oils sat on the tile next to the tub.

*Home.* This was her home. Her mind worked to wrap around the enormity of it all. Cara had been raised in a wealthy family and had enjoyed a certain level of luxury, but nothing like the opulence that surrounded her.

"I'm overwhelmed," she said, turning to face him. "It's more beautiful that you described."

"I can't wait to show you my country and my people," he replied as he drew her into his embrace. "I hope you will love them as I know they will come to love you."

She smiled tremulously. "I can't remember ever being this happy in my entire life."

He leaned down and touched his lips to hers in a soft, sweet kiss. "And it is my wish that you will always be happy here. And now, are you hungry? I could get somebody to get us a snack."

She shook her head. "No. The meal your chef cooked for dinner on the plane was wonderful, and I'm still quite full."

"Then, I suggest we call it a night. We have breakfast arranged for seven in the morning. I took the liberty of ordering nightwear for you, knowing that we'd be arriving late and might not want to unpack. In the closet on the left in the bathroom are some things for you."

He was a man of many surprises, Cara thought as she went back into the bathroom and into the closet he'd indicated. There she found hanging a lovely red silk nightgown, but it wasn't his thoughtfulness in arranging for a new nightgown that touched her.

Next to where the dress hung, there was a shelf, on which sat a bud vase with a single perfect red rose. There was a note tied to it, and the note read:

What a terrible place the world would be without flowers!
It would be a heart without a soul.

She knew the words well, for she had written them to him in a letter when she'd spoken of her love of flowers.

The fact that he'd remembered her sentiment and given them back to her with a lovely rose, filled her heart with a deepening love for the man she had married.

She changed from her clothes to the nightgown, loving the way the elegant silk caressed her skin. Although just that morning Omar had made love to her in the shower, she hungered for his touch as if it had been months, years, since they had last been intimate.

With the rose in her hand, she entered the bedroom, where the lights were dim, candles burned, music tinkled faintly and the fragrance of incense filled the air.

Beyond the wispy veils that surrounded the bed, she saw her husband, and her heart stepped up its rhythm at the beauty of his male form stretched out against white sheets.

"You are amazing," she said as she parted the veils around the bed and crawled up next to him. She held the rose to his nose, allowing him to smell the intoxicating fragrance. "How did you remember the words I wrote to you?"

He smiled. "I remember many of the words you wrote to me." He slid one of his hands through her hair, caressing the strands as if they were fine silk. "You always spoke in such beautiful words."

"I used a lot of beautiful quotes to speak what was in my heart. So many people through the ages have been eloquent when speaking about beauty and dreams and love."

She suddenly realized he hadn't spoken of love, not one time, not in the days they had spent together in Texas, not when he'd proposed marriage and not since the ceremony that had made them man and wife.

Of course, she hadn't told him that she loved him, either. Her love for him was too new to speak of, an ever-deepening emotion that continued to thrill her.

Deep inside, she knew the real reason she hadn't spoken of her love for him was that it didn't seem right to tell him she loved him before she told him of her true identity.

*You should tell him the truth now,* a little voice whispered inside her head, but at that moment his lips sought hers in a kiss of such passion, such desire, it instantly overwhelmed any need she felt for such a confession.

Later, as she drifted off to sleep with the exotic scents and sounds of her new home surrounding her, she told herself she would tell Omar the truth tomorrow. And hopefully, he would not only forgive her, but would take her in his arms and tell her he didn't care what her real name was, that he loved her and only her.

Morning crept into her consciousness with the sound of birds singing sweet morning songs, and a gentle breeze caressing her naked body as it whispered through the gauzy curtains that surrounded the bed.

She opened her eyes to see Omar, fully dressed and standing at the opened French doors that led out into a private garden.

She took the opportunity to study the man she had married, admiring the breadth of his shoulders beneath the white suit jacket, the slender hips and muscular legs hugged by the white slacks.

His dark hair gleamed in a shaft of sunlight that found its way to where he stood, and she remembered clutching his hair, gripping his shoulders and clinging to him the night before as he'd made love to her.

She was struck once again by the sounds of birds. Their different songs filled the air.

"What a lovely way to wake up," she said.

Omar turned from the doorway and walked over to the bed, where he pulled aside one of the veil curtains and smiled at her. "Yes," he agreed. "There's nothing better than awakening to a gorgeous naked woman in your bed."

She fought the desire to pull the sheet up over her, a new confidence flowing through her as she saw the pleasure that lit his eyes. "Silly, I was talking about the bird songs," she replied.

"Ah yes, the birds. This garden has an aviary that my father had built when he was Sheik of Gaspar. He's something of a bird lover."

"I can't wait to meet him."

"And so you will, in half an hour," Omar replied.

"Half an hour!" Cara shot up and scrambled from

the bed. "Why didn't you tell me it was so late?" she exclaimed as she ran for the bathroom.

She was surprised to discover the clothes she had brought with her from Texas were now hanging neatly in the closet. Her underclothing was on a shelf and her toiletries were on the countertop next to one of the two sinks.

She took a fast shower, then dressed in a long-sleeved, lightweight beige dress. As she applied just a touch of makeup, she was surprised to discover she was nervous about meeting Omar's father.

She knew from Omar's letters and from their conversations that he held an enormous amount of love and respect for his father, and it was important to her that Omar's father approve of her.

When she finally stepped out of the bathroom, Omar's eyes lit with pleasure at the sight of her, and she knew the choice of the conservative dress had been correct.

"Ah, Elizabeth, you look lovely. My father's heart will be stolen by you as quickly as my own heart was."

His words soothed her nerves and, as they left their private quarters, she was even more grateful when he took her hand.

"Does Rashad live here at the palace?" she asked, as they walked down the long corridor that led toward the opposite wing where his father resided. She hadn't seen the charming little man since they had landed at the airport.

"Rashad has a comfortable apartment in another of the palace buildings. However, I imagine he will be at breakfast. Rashad is like a member of the royal family and is usually a part of any gathering."

Guards also stood on either side of the door that led to Sheik Abdul Al Abdar's quarters. They bowed respectfully to both Omar and Cara, then opened the door to allow them entry.

Rashad met them just inside the door, his face wreathed with a smile as he greeted them. "Good morning to the newlyweds," he exclaimed. "You both look positively splendid this morning."

"Thank you, Rashad," Cara replied, as always finding herself smiling when in his presence.

"Your family awaits you in the dining room," he said to Omar.

Cara looked at Omar curiously. His *family?* The word implied more than his father, and she didn't know Omar had other family members.

She suddenly realized she knew very little about Sheik Abdul's personal life, although she knew Omar's mother had died in childbirth. Perhaps Omar had aunts and uncles who would be eating breakfast with them.

Sheik Abdul's quarters were laid out much like Omar's quarters, although smaller and less grand. As they walked through the living-room area, Omar squeezed her hand, as if knowing her nerves were stretched taut. She cast him a grateful smile.

They entered a dining room, not as large or formal

as the one in Omar's quarters. Seated at the table were a man and three women, all of whom stood when they entered.

If Sheik Abdul had been in a lineup of a hundred men, Cara could have picked him out easily as Omar's father. Their build was the same—tall with powerful shoulders and arms.

Omar had taken from his father not only his build but also his sharply honed facial features and striking handsomeness.

"Ah, my son." Sheik Abdul embraced Omar, then turned to Cara, his eyes warm with welcome. "And my new daughter. Welcome," he exclaimed as he hugged Cara, as well. "Come and sit." He released Cara and gestured toward the table. "I'm starving."

Omar laughed. "Some things never change. Father, you're always starving." He took Cara's elbow and led her to where the three women stood looking at them both expectantly. "Elizabeth, may I present Hayfa, Jahara and Malika, my father's wives."

If Omar had entertained any doubts about the woman he'd chosen to make his wife, the last of them would have vanished during the breakfast meal.

He watched in satisfaction and pride as Elizabeth charmed his father with her intelligence, her grace and her warmth. The conversation was as good and varied as the food that was served.

He also knew that Elizabeth had made conquests in Jahara and Malika, the younger of his father's two wives. They sat side by side, gazing wide-eyed at Elizabeth as if she were a wonderfully exotic creature. But they smiled at her often, smiles that promised the hand of friendship.

Hayfa was another matter. The older woman sat at his father's right hand, watching Omar's bride with suspicious eyes. She was the only one of the wives with her face half-veiled and her hair covered.

It had been Hayfa who had raised Omar. Intensely maternal, fiercely loving, she was a curious mix of woman, warrior and girl. While she loved many things from the United States, including Tom Cruise movies and the music of Elvis Presley, she had campaigned for Omar to marry a woman from Gaspar.

Omar caught her eye and winked at her, then grinned as she sent him a scathing glare. Elizabeth would have a challenge in winning Hayfa's respect and affection, but he had no doubt eventually Elizabeth would prevail.

"I think a party is in order, to officially introduce your new bride," Sheik Abdul said while they were lingering over coffee.

"A dance!" Malika replied, her dark eyes lighting with excitement. "We can have it in the grand ballroom on Friday night."

"Friday night is too soon," Hayfa replied. "It would take at least a week to pull something together."

"Oh yes, Omar, please say yes." Jahara looked eagerly at Omar.

He glanced at Elizabeth and smiled. "I think that's

a fine idea. We'll plan something for a week from Saturday night. We'll make it a day of celebration to honor my new wife."

"Please, that isn't necessary—" Elizabeth began to protest, but Omar held up a hand to still her.

"I've made up my mind and it will be done," he said. "Besides, I have yet to dance with my wife, and that's something I look forward to with great anticipation." He smiled at Jahara and Malika. "And I am sure my father's esteemed wives will be more than happy to see to it that my bride has an appropriate dress for the occasion."

"I don't want to put anyone to any trouble," Elizabeth protested again.

"Trouble?" Sheik Abdul laughed. "My wives live to shop. Trust me, it would not be a problem for them to take you to their favorite stores."

"How about tomorrow?" Malika asked. "We could have lunch out and make a day of it."

Elizabeth looked at Omar and it was obvious she was a bit overwhelmed. He smiled at his stepmothers. "We'll let you know later today if those plans will work for tomorrow. And now, as pleasant as this has been, I'd like to give Elizabeth a tour of the palace and grounds. We arrived too late last evening for her to see much of anything."

They bid his family goodbye, and he and Elizabeth left the dining room. "My father was quite taken with you," Omar said the moment they walked out of the quarters.

"He seems to be a wonderful man," she replied.

"He is one of the finest men on earth. Kind and wise. He was not only a good ruler for Gaspar, he was also a wonderful father."

A tiny frown worried the skin across her forehead as he led her down the grand staircase. "I think your stepmother hates me."

Omar laughed and took her hand in his. "Hayfa doesn't hate anyone. She merely enjoys giving the illusion of being fierce. She's the eldest of the three wives and was the first that my father married. It was Hayfa who raised me, and she's perhaps a bit too protective where I'm concerned."

When they reached the bottom of the stairs, Omar led her into a large reception room. "We call this the throne room," he explained.

At the far end was a throne, flanked by flags. Most of the rest of the room was taken up by chairs facing the throne area. "This is where I meet with the people to discuss problems and issues that concern them."

"When did your father marry Malika and Jahara?" she asked as they left the throne room.

"Father married all three women in the year following my mother's death and my birth." Omar realized she was struggling to understand the idea of a man having three wives. "He told me once that he married Hayfa because he needed a mother for his son. She had been a friend of my mother's, and he knew she had a maternal heart and would love me as her own."

They entered a huge ballroom with elaborate crystal chandeliers and walls covered with silk embroideries. "This is where we'll have the dance on Saturday night," he explained, then continued on the original subject. "Father married Malika several months after he'd married Hayfa. He was drawn to Malika's quick wit and sharp intelligence. He knew she was a woman he could talk to about any subject."

"And Jahara?"

"Jahara became his third wife a month after he married Malika. He married Jahara because she made him laugh. She's filled with life and spirit and has a wonderful sense of humor." He recognized by her expression that she was disturbed by his words, and he drew her into an embrace. "I was far luckier than my father. I found one woman who has all those qualities."

"But what about love? How can your father love three women?" she asked, her green eyes gazing at him curiously.

He released his hold on her. "Elizabeth, the concept of love is different for a sheik than for a normal man."

"I don't understand. What exactly does that mean?" she asked.

"It means that you should be a good and dutiful wife so I'll never have the need to marry another one," he teased.

"Your Highness?" Rashad appeared in the doorway of the ballroom. "I'm sorry to interrupt, but Moham-

mad Dubar is on the phone and says he has an update
on the oil negotiations."

Omar turned to Elizabeth with an apologetic smile.
"I'm afraid I must take this call. Rashad, would you
mind showing Elizabeth the formal gardens?"

Rashad smiled at her. "It would be my honor."

"Good." Omar kissed her forehead. "I'll catch up
with you later."

As he left Rashad and Elizabeth, Omar hoped there
would be no more talk of love.

He'd followed Elizabeth's exploits before marrying
her, had known she had a reputation as something of
a jet-setter, and while he'd been surprised to discover
her a virgin, he'd thought she would understand that
he had married her for many reasons, but love hadn't
been one of them.

## Chapter 9

Cara had been in a mild state of shock from the moment Omar introduced her to his father's three wives. All the time she had dreamed of living in Gaspar, in all the letters Omar had written to her, she'd never imagined, and he'd never told her, that polygamy was a way of life here.

She'd been worried that he'd be angry when she told him the truth about her identity, but now she had a new worry. If she upset him or made him angry, he could just go out and marry another woman.

Had her mother been right, after all? Had she jumped into this relationship, this new country, without thinking about all the changes that would take place in her life? Had she married Omar for all the wrong reasons?

Her heart answered the question. *Absolutely not.* She loved Omar. Every moment of every day that she spent with him, her love only grew more profound.

But, because she loved him so much, she couldn't imagine sharing him with another woman. The very idea was alien to her.

"You are troubled." Rashad's voice broke into her thoughts as he led her toward an enormous set of doors.

He looked around, as if checking to see if anyone else was nearby, then smiled at her. "Do not let Hayfa's silence and sourness frighten you. She has the bark of a dog, but the dog doesn't bite."

Cara couldn't help but laugh at his description of the older woman. "I have to confess, I found her a bit daunting."

"She likes to pretend to be daunting." Rashad opened the door, and together they stepped out into the bright sunshine of midmorning. "But she has a good heart."

The air was heavily scented with the fragrance of a thousand flowers, and Cara's breath caught at the beauty before her. For as far as her eyes could see there were plants and trees, flowers and shrubs.

"Sheik Abdul created the gardens as a wedding present for his wife, Omar's mother," Rashad said, as they began to walk down a path through the center of the garden. They were surrounded by the most lush, colorful blossoming flowers she'd ever seen.

"Did you know her?" she asked.

Rashad nodded. "Yes, I was working for Sheik Abdul when he met her."

"Tell me about her," she said, welcoming a change in topic that momentarily made her forget the fact that at any moment her husband might decide to take a second wife.

"Antonia was her name."

"Antonia? So she wasn't from Gaspar?"

"No. Sheik Abdul met her on a trip to Greece. She was the daughter of an ambassador and was one of the most beautiful women I've ever seen in my life. She had beautiful dark hair and black eyes that held a wealth of emotion and warmth. Sheik Abdul was besotted with her the moment he lay eyes on her, and she seemed to be equally besotted with him."

"And so they married," Cara said, and paused to smell a brilliant purple flower she didn't recognize.

"Indeed, there were days of celebration all over Gaspar during the week of the royal wedding. The people of Gaspar love a good romance and particularly love any reason for a celebration."

Rashad motioned to a stone bench in front of a beautiful fountain. "Would you like to sit for a few minutes?"

She nodded, and they sat side by side, enjoying a few minutes of silence broken only by the burbling of the water in the fountain.

"This was one of her favorite places," Rashad said, finally breaking the peaceful quiet. "She came here almost every day to sit and enjoy the tranquillity of the garden. She said whenever she sat here she felt surrounded by Sheik Abdul's love."

"That's nice. How long were she and the sheik married before she passed away?"

"They had two years together before she died. They were wonderful years both for Sheik Abdul and for the country."

"And she died in childbirth?"

Rashad nodded, his expression sad. "She told nobody that she had a severe heart condition and that her doctor had warned her against pregnancy. She was determined to give Sheik Abdul the son he longed for, and she did, but at the greatest cost."

Again they were silent, and Cara found herself thinking of the woman who had been Omar's mother, a woman who had sacrificed her life for her son.

Had Sheik Abdul loved her with all his heart, with all his soul, or had his love been limited somehow because he was a sheik? She thought of Omar's words—that sheiks loved differently than other men. What had he meant? And what did that mean for her?

"You liked her," Cara finally observed, disturbed by her thoughts.

"Very much," Rashad replied. "I don't think anyone disliked her. She was not only kind, but she brought to the palace life and laughter and a kind of magic that died when she died."

"And Sheik Abdul?"

"Withdrew into privacy for two weeks and has never mentioned her name again. Within a month he married Hayfa, who had been caretaking for Omar since his birth. And the rest, as they say, is history."

"What about you, Rashad? Have you ever been in love?" she asked, curious about his life beyond his position as Omar's personal assistant.

"Once…long ago." His dark eyes grew soft and his mouth curved into a faint smile. "I was very young, and she was very pretty. She ended up marrying a wealthy businessman from the United States and now lives in California."

Cara placed her hand on his arm. "I'm so sorry."

"Ah, it was a long time ago, and besides, I have been subtly courting a woman who works at the palace as a maid." To her surprise his cheeks darkened with the stain of a blush. "Although, things have been progressing rather slowly. We have coffee together early every morning, but there are usually others there, as well."

"Have you asked her out?" Cara asked.

He shook his head. "I'm unsure how she would react to such a request."

"Nothing ventured, nothing gained," she replied. "What's her name?"

"Jane." He smiled at her look of surprise. "She is not originally from Gaspar. She, too, is from the United States. She married a man from Gaspar many years ago and came here to live. Ten years ago her husband was killed in a car accident, but she chose to remain here instead of returning to Montana, where she is from." He cleared his throat. "But enough about me. Shall we walk some more? There is still much of the gardens to see."

She nodded, and together they stood and began to walk again. As they walked, he pointed out different species of flowers, each grouping meticulously planned to show their particular brilliance and color.

Still, despite the beauty that surrounded her, despite Rashad's interesting commentary about the gardens and the various flowers, Cara's mind continued to whirl with the knowledge that Omar's father had three wives.

Would there come a time when Omar tired of her and sought a new diversion, a new wife? When she finally mustered the courage to tell him the truth about herself, would he, in anger, choose another bride?

As much as she was growing to love him, she didn't think she could stand being one of several wives. She wanted, needed from him the kind of love regular men felt, the kind of love that was a commitment between two people, a promise of fidelity and respect.

"I don't mean to intrude, but you still seem troubled by something. Is there anything I can do to help?" Rashad asked, his eyes gazing at her sharply as they continued their tour through the gardens.

"I'm still trying to digest the idea of a man having three wives," she said truthfully. "In none of our letters and conversations did Omar mention to me that his father had more than one wife."

"Then Hayfa, Jahara and Malika must have been a big surprise," he observed.

"That's certainly an understatement," she replied dryly. "Now I find myself wondering if and when Omar might decide to follow in his father's footsteps and take another wife."

"That isn't likely to happen," Rashad said with a smile.

"Why not?" Cara eyed him curiously.

"First and foremost for the obvious reasons." Rashad's dark eyes twinkled merrily. "He will never find a woman as beautiful, as charming and as perfect for him as you."

Cara laughed. "There is an exceptionally large chunk of malarkey in you, Rashad."

He laughed, as well. "All right, then I'll tell you another reason why he's not likely to take another wife. The laws changed some twenty years ago, and polygamy is now against the law."

Cara was surprised by the relief that fluttered through her, a relief tempered with a touch of irritation that Omar hadn't mentioned the same little fact.

When she saw him, she would show him just how good and dutiful she could be.

Omar was on his way to the formal gardens to find his wife, when he ran into Hayfa in one of the corridors.

"Mother," he said respectfully, then leaned forward to kiss her on the forehead.

Her face was no longer covered, and she smiled with pleasure as he released her. "My son, it's so good to have you back where you belong. I miss seeing your face when you're away."

"You just miss me because when I'm gone you have nobody to yell at," he replied teasingly.

"That's not true. I regularly yell at Malika and Jahara. They often forget their age and act like teenagers."

Omar laughed and took her arm, and together they walked down the corridor. "So, tell me, Mother, what did you think of my new bride?"

Hayfa hesitated before answering, as if schooling her thoughts. "She's very beautiful. It's easy to see why she captured your eye." She said the words thinly, letting him sense her vague disapproval.

"You didn't raise me to be so shallow that I would marry a woman for her looks alone," he chided. "She has a good heart, Hayfa. If you would just give her a chance, she's bright and funny and spirited."

"Yes, I know of her spirited nature. The gossip columns have occasionally mentioned her spirited exploits."

Unfortunately, Omar had no argument against this fact. There were times when he himself struggled with the characterization of Elizabeth Fiona he'd gleaned through gossip magazines and the quite different Elizabeth Fiona he'd gotten to know through her letters and in spending time with her.

"One could say that I was equally spirited," he finally replied. "I believe on more than one occasion I've been written up in those same gossip columns."

"It's different for a man," she replied stiffly.

He laughed and gave her a quick hug. "And you are occasionally an old-fashioned frump." He released her and grew more serious. "Be kind to her, Hayfa. She's left her family, her country and all that she knows to be my wife. Your friendship and approval here could make things easier on her."

She reached up and placed her palm on the side of his face, her eyes warm with love. "I only want to see you happy, and if she makes you happy, I will respect that."

"She does make me happy."

Hayfa nodded. "Then, I will be kind."

Omar kissed her again, then left her and went in search of his wife.

He found her with Rashad in the gardens. He saw them before they saw him, and he paused to drink in the sight of the woman who would be at his side at the end of each day, the woman who would eventually bear his children and grow old with him.

She was laughing at something Rashad had said, and for a moment he desperately wished he had a camera to capture forever the sheer joy that lit her lovely features.

Her dark brown hair shone in the sunlight, sparkling with just a hint of red highlights, and he knew her green eyes would be twinkling.

Desire hit him right in the middle of his gut. It was not just a desire to take her to bed and stroke her nakedness, lose himself in her. Rather, it was also a desire to see her laugh often, to never be the cause of tears in her eyes.

The inertia that had momentarily gripped him broke, and he was suddenly eager to join in the conversation, to get close enough to see the sparkle of her eyes.

He hurried toward them, surprised when he reached them and Elizabeth bowed deeply.

"Your Highness," she murmured with her head kept down. "How good of you to join us." She glanced up at him just quickly enough for him to catch a glimpse of those teasing, flirtatious eyes. "Is there anything I can do to please you? I await your command."

Omar cast a look to Rashad, who shrugged in equal bewilderment. "Elizabeth, what are you doing?"

Again he saw a flash of emerald eyes, then she returned her gaze to his feet. "I am attempting to be a good and dutiful wife so that you will not see the need to marry another woman."

Rashad, obviously recognizing he was not needed, nodded quickly to Omar, then scurried away.

Omar returned his gaze to her, amusement rippling through him. "This presents a wealth of possibilities to me. Perhaps we could return to our quarters and you can show me just how good and dutiful you can be."

She raised a hand and smacked him lightly on the chest, her eyes holding the light of indignation. "You are a wicked man not to tell me that polygamy is no longer practiced here in Gaspar."

She started to smack him again, but he caught her hand and laughingly pulled her to his chest. "I thought you knew."

"I didn't know until Rashad told me a little while ago. It was mean of you to let me worry for even one single moment that I might have to share you with another woman."

"And you would mind that so much?" he asked.

Her eyes flashed darkly. "I don't like to share," she said as she wound her arms around his neck.

"Good, because neither do I," he replied, electrified by the fierceness in her tone and the sweet press of her body against his.

She unwound her arms and stepped back from him. "Good, now that we have that settled, perhaps you'll show me the rest of the gardens."

"I would be delighted." He took her arm in his, and together they walked at a leisurely pace. "Have you given any thought to your plans for tomorrow? Have you decided to go shopping with my father's wives?"

"I didn't want to plan anything until I spoke with you. We haven't really discussed what our daily schedule will be, what my duties and responsibilities as your wife are. Other than acting as hostess at palace functions. And there must be more than that for me to do," she protested. "I don't want to be simply a decoration on your arm, Omar."

"You can plan menus with the cook for our evening meals and oversee the housekeeping staff."

He was surprised to see a frown dashing across

her face. "Those aren't the kinds of things I'm talking about," she replied. "I can do those, but I want to do more. I'd like to get involved in some charity work, either work on existing programs or create new ones to take care of the needs of the people of Gaspar."

She continued to amaze him. How had he ever entertained the possibility that she might be shallow or frivolous? He tightened his grip on her arm, pleasure sweeping through him as he realized she truly wanted to be a part of his life, a part of Gaspar.

"If you're interested in doing charity work, then the person to speak with is Hayfa. She's been coordinating several charities for many years. And speaking of Hayfa, if you'd like to go shopping tomorrow, that works fine with my schedule. Unfortunately, my day will be quite busy with meetings."

"Then, I guess I'm going shopping," she replied. Again she frowned. "Omar—"

"Sheik Omar," Rashad called from the distance, interrupting whatever Elizabeth had been about to say.

Omar looked at Elizabeth. "I had hoped to be able to spend time today showing you around, but because it is my first day back in the country, there is a lot of business to attend to. I apologize."

"Don't apologize," she replied, and smiled the lovely smile that never failed to light a flame inside him. "I knew what I was getting into when I married you, Omar. I knew you would have enormous demands on your time and attention."

"I'm a lucky man, darling," he said, and kissed her

on her temple. "Feel free to wander wherever you wish within the palace, and perhaps day after tomorrow we can take a tour of the countryside."

For the first time in his life, as Omar left her there amid the blossoming flowers, he was almost sorry he was a sheik. For just a moment he wished he were nothing more than a simple man who could spend the day in the company of his lovely wife.

# Chapter 10

Cara stood before the mirror in the luxurious bathroom, giving herself a final once-over as she waited for Omar's stepmothers to meet her for a day of shopping.

She was nervous about the day ahead, but nothing could detract from the happiness in her heart. After her brief tour of the formal gardens the day before, when Omar had left her, she'd returned here to their private quarters, and had met with the staff, whom she found respectful yet friendly.

After meeting with them, she wandered from room to room, familiarizing herself with the layout and attempting to make the opulent, grand place feel like home.

It felt like home only when Omar had returned and

they shared a simple dinner in the breakfast nook. Afterward they sat in their private little garden and she listened as he told her about his activities of the day.

Over and over she reminded herself that she had to tell him the truth, that each day that passed only made her lie worse. A dozen times the night before, she'd tried to bring the words of truth to her lips, but as she'd seen the gentleness in his eyes and the tender smile curving his lips, the words simply refused to come.

She turned away from her reflection, unexpected tears burning her eyes. It had all begun as something of a lark, but now it had become painful.

The happiness she'd found with Omar felt fragile and she was afraid that by telling him the truth, that happiness would be shattered, never to be put back together again.

As she left the master bath, she heard a knock at the door. "I'll get it," she told the maid, who nodded and returned to her task of dusting.

She opened the door and was surprised to see Rashad. "Rashad! I was expecting Omar's stepmothers."

"They are awaiting you in the car," he explained. "I am to accompany you on your shopping trip today."

"Oh, I'm so glad," she replied. "At least I'll be assured of one friendly face."

"Surely you aren't nervous," he exclaimed. "You are the wife of our sheik. They should be nervous about spending time with you."

Cara grabbed his thin arm and gave it a grateful squeeze as they left the quarters. "Rashad, what on earth would I do without you?"

"I think you would be just fine," he replied. "I have a feeling you are a woman of strength and purpose. You will be an asset not only to Sheik Omar, but to the country, as well."

She nodded, although she didn't feel strong at all. She felt weak and weepy and filled with remorse. She wished desperately that she could go back in time, back to that moment when Omar had appeared on her doorstep—she would immediately tell him the truth about everything.

She had allowed her desire to have someone of her own to override everything else, and what worried her more than anything was the fear that the price she would eventually pay would be enormous.

The car was a huge limo, and as she and Rashad approached, she saw Hayfa, Jahara and Malika already inside.

"I will be up front with the driver," he said. "And you will be fine." He opened the door to admit her into the back with the rest of the women.

"Please, Elizabeth, sit here," Jahara said, patting the seat next to her. Elizabeth slid onto the seat facing Hayfa and Malika.

"Good morning to you all," she said, noting that this morning Hayfa didn't have her face covered.

"Good morning to you," Malika replied and smiled. "We're going to have such fun. We're taking you to our favorite dress shop, then to our favorite restaurant for lunch."

"Where you will certainly eat too much, then complain for the rest of the afternoon," Hayfa said to the younger woman.

Malika seemed to take no offense. She laughed and winked one of her dark, beautiful eyes at Cara. "She's just jealous because my food does not ultimately rest on my hips."

Hayfa sniffed and turned her attention out the window. Jahara touched Cara's hand and smiled. "Tell us about Texas," she said. "I hear it is a state filled with strong, handsome cowboys."

Cara laughed. "Well, not everybody who lives in Texas is a cowboy," she explained. For the remainder of the ride Cara told them about her home state. She described to them the ranch where she had been born and raised, and in the back of her mind she wondered if eventually she would return there, divorced and disgraced by the lie she had perpetrated.

By the time the car pulled to a halt, she was feeling a bit more at ease. She'd even managed to coax a small smile from Hayfa.

There was nothing like a shopping spree to bond women together, she thought as the four of them got out of the car and entered the establishment simply named Fadoul's.

They appeared to be the only shoppers, and it wasn't until Cara saw the guards on either side of the door that she realized there would be no other shoppers as long as the sheik's wife was inside.

A tall, thin man with a full beard greeted them, bowing so deeply Cara was afraid he might brush his pointy nose to the floor. "It is my honor to welcome you to my humble establishment," he said. "It is my great honor to be of service to Sheik Abdar's new bride. Please let me know if there is anything I can do to assist you in—"

"Enough, Fadoul," Hayfa exclaimed impatiently. "We have come to shop, not to listen to your orating skills."

Cara nearly giggled aloud at the look of shock that crossed Fadoul's face. "My new daughter-in-law requires a dress for a celebration next Saturday night. I trust you have something suitable?"

Fadoul bowed once again. "I will leave you in the hands of my wife, who has served you all so many times before." He disappeared behind a curtain near the back of the shop, and a moment later an attractive women approached them.

"Hayfa, it is good to see you again," she said. "And Jahara and Malika, it's always a pleasure to serve you." She turned to Cara and smiled. "I am Safia and I am pleased to meet you. My husband said that Sheik Omar's new bride would be easy to dress, and I see what he means. You are quite beautiful."

"Thank you," Cara murmured.

With introductions over, the women began to explore the clothes that hung on racks and on displays around the shop. Most of the clothing was of Eastern fashion although there was some Western wear mixed in.

Cara decided the best thing she could do for the celebration on Saturday night was to wear something traditional to Gaspar. Hayfa explained to her that the traditional dress of Gaspar was called a *jalabiya,* a long-sleeved, floor-length gown with matching haremlike pants beneath.

Safia showed Cara the selection, and as she thumbed through the various garments, Cara found herself appreciating the simple yet sophisticated look of the gowns. There was a wide variety of colors, with use of gems and embroidery for decorative touches.

"I have been working on a *jalabiya* that I have in the back room," Safia said. "Perhaps you would like to see it."

"All right," she agreed. As the other women chose clothing to try on and disappeared into the dressing rooms, Cara followed Safia to the back room.

She saw the *jalabiya* immediately and knew it was what she wanted to wear for the celebration. The fabric was a deep, royal purple silk and the neck was encrusted with tiny seed pearls.

"Oh, Safia, it's beautiful," she exclaimed. "And you could have it finished in time for the celebration a week from Saturday night?"

"If you try it on now, we can do a fitting and I can assure you I'll have it finished in time."

Cara had just slipped the gown on, when Hayfa

appeared in the doorway. "A good choice," she said with approval. "Not only do you honor the women of Gaspar by wearing traditional dress, you honor all people of Gaspar by choosing a dress of the royal colors."

Cara smiled at the older woman. "As long as Omar likes it, I'll be happy."

Safia left the room for a moment, and Cara was aware of Hayfa's gaze lingering on her with speculation. "You love my son?"

Cara held her gaze. "More than anyone I've ever loved in my life."

"I've studied the gossip columns, have seen some reports of your love life and spirited nature. A sheik needs a wife who is not fodder for gossip, a woman who has a good head on her shoulders and will support him through the good times and bad."

Cara knew the gossip Hayfa had read had been about Fiona, not her. A quiet, unobtrusive teacher's life was hardly worth reporting about. But how could she explain that to Hayfa when she hadn't yet told Omar?

"Hayfa, I am not the same woman that you read about in the papers. Things happen…people change. And all I want to do now is build a future with Omar."

Just then, Malika and Jahara entered the back room, exclaiming with excitement over Cara's dress and showing her what they had picked out.

The morning passed swiftly as they finished shopping for matching shoes and accessories. It didn't take long for Cara to get a sense of each woman's personality.

Jahara was a ray of sunshine, bright and bubbly and, from what the other two explained, an expert at belly dancing. Malika was a bit more serious but no less friendly. Then there was Hayfa, who mothered the other two with a touch of amused indulgence.

The relationship the three of them shared was obviously strong and based on mutual affection and friendship and Cara found herself wondering why three lovely, capable women would choose to share one man's love.

It was over lunch that she asked the three what it was like to be married to the same man.

"Forgive me for being nosy, but I've never known anyone practicing polygamy," she said.

"You must understand that it was a different time, a different generation, when we all married Sheik Abdul," Malika explained. "Before Sheik Abdul came to power, Gaspar was a poor nation. We sat on the biggest oil fields in the Middle East, but were doing nothing to utilize that resource."

"We were also a nation that had far more women than men, and if a woman didn't marry, she starved," Hayfa continued. "So, a man took as many wives as he could afford to take care of."

The entire concept was alien to Cara, but she understood the difference in the time and the culture. "Still, it must be difficult emotionally to know that you share Sheik Abdul's love among the three of you."

Hayfa smiled ruefully. "You Westerners rely far too heavily on emotion when it comes to love. I knew when I married Sheik Abdul that he was not offering me love. He needed a mother for Omar, and he knew I was barren and would never have children of my own."

"Sheiks are taught to use their heads, not their hearts," Malika explained. "Love is an emotion that weakens a man, and sheiks cannot be weak. Women are respected, admired and desired, and for us, that is enough."

Cara nodded, but what they didn't understand was that respect, admiration and desire would never be enough for her. She had to believe that Omar Al Abdar was a sheik in touch with his heart, and that his heart loved her.

"Have I told you how lovely you look tonight?" Omar asked his wife as he drew her into his arms for a dance.

"Several times, but feel free to tell me again." Her gorgeous eyes shone brightly as she gazed up at him.

He felt her happiness thrumming inside his veins, warming him from his head to his toes. It was a familiar feeling, one that had been with him for the past two weeks, whenever he'd been in her company.

"You look absolutely stunning," he said. And it was true. The deep purple *jalabiya* fit her to perfection, hugging the curves that had become so familiar to him and deepening the shade of her emerald eyes.

"Thank you," she replied.

He pulled her closer, the scent of her stirring his senses as they glided across the dance floor. As he held her tightly against him, he eyed their surroundings with satisfaction.

The celebration to introduce Elizabeth as his wife had been an unqualified success, although it was now beginning to wind down.

The menu had been an international one, with French cuisine being served right next to Greek pastries. The guest list was an international one, as well, with ambassadors from several countries in attendance along with other dignitaries.

Yes, it had been a huge success, largely due to Elizabeth's natural charm and grace—qualities that already had most of the people of Gaspar in love with her.

In the two weeks, she had done everything she could to make herself visible and accessible to the people. She had visited the sick at a local hospital, read to the elderly in a nursing home, and had even managed to win over Hayfa.

"You've become very quiet, Your Highness," she said, those bewitching eyes of hers once again connecting with his.

"I was just thinking about what a wonderfully intelligent man I am," he replied.

"Really? And what brought you to such a startling conclusion?" she asked.

"You," he replied. "I must be wonderfully intelligent to have married you."

Her eyes, so expressive, misted slightly. "Do you mean that, Omar?" she asked softly, but the softness in her tone was belied by the intensity of her gaze. "Are you happy with me? Would you marry me all over again?"

As always, he was oddly touched by the streak of insecurity she occasionally displayed. "How a woman as beautiful, as giving and as special as you could ever doubt that I would marry you again is beyond me," he replied. "I would be a fool not to marry you again, and trust me, my love, I am nobody's fool."

She lay her head back on his chest, and he breathed deeply of the familiar scent of her hair. There had been many pleasant surprises for him over the course of the past two weeks of marriage, so many things he hadn't considered.

Aside from the fact that he had a warm, willing woman in his bed each night, he'd come to enjoy their early conversations over morning coffee. He liked the fact that his living quarters now retained the scent of her in every room, just as her laughter so often filled the chambers of his heart.

When he'd thought in the abstract of being married, he'd never considered how much he would enjoy sharing his life, his thoughts, his dreams with another person.

"Now that the oil negotiations are no longer an issue, I'm hoping to spend more time with you," he said. The negotiations had concluded the day before, with the signing of new agreements and the promise of continuing prosperity for the people in Gaspar.

"That would be very nice," she replied, looking up at him again. "Although I'm not complaining, it doesn't seem like I've seen much of you."

Again he tightened his arm around her. "Unfortunately, there has been too much business lately and not enough pleasure, but hopefully things will quiet down now and I'll have some leisure time."

He smiled as she stifled a yawn. "And now, I think perhaps it's time for the sheik and his wife to call it a night. It's been a long day, and, as I recall, you had one of your nightmares last night."

Her cheeks colored. "And I'm sorry for waking you up," she replied.

"I'm not sorry that you woke me up," he replied. "I'm just glad I can be there to hold you and soothe you when those night terrors hit." Again her eyes grew moist, and he thought it was probably a result of too much party and too little sleep.

"I will have Rashad take you to our quarters, and I will be up in just a little while. There are some people I need to say goodbye to."

He gestured to his aide, who stood nearby. Rashad was instantly by their side. "Rashad, would you please escort Elizabeth to our quarters?"

"It would be my pleasure," Rashad replied.

Omar watched as Rashad and Elizabeth made their way toward the doors to the ballroom. It took them several minutes to reach the doors because she stopped again and again to speak to people, to shake a hand and offer a smile.

"She is delightful."

Omar turned to see his father standing next to him. "Yes, she is, isn't she."

"She will bring good things to the palace, things like laughter and joy."

Omar smiled. "She's already brought that to me."

Sheik Abdul nodded. "She reminds me of your mother."

Omar looked at his father in surprise. It was the first time he could ever remember his father even mentioning Omar's mother. But before he could say or ask anything more, Sheik Abdul walked away.

It was some time later that Omar sat at his desk in his official office, checking to make certain there was nothing that needed to be attended to before he joined Elizabeth in their private quarters.

He leaned back in his desk chair, thinking of the mother he had never known. What little he knew about her, he'd learned from Hayfa and Rashad, not from his father. What he found even stranger than his father's mention of his mother was the wistfulness he'd thought he heard in his father's voice.

"Nothing more than my imagination," he murmured aloud as he checked his wristwatch. It was nearly two, and he was exhausted. But, of course, not too exhausted to hold his wife in his arms, fill his senses with her and make tender, passionate love to her.

On impulse, he opened his desk drawer and took out the picture of Elizabeth, the photo that had been taken so many years ago at the cotillion where she'd first bewitched him.

Before he'd gone to Texas to claim her as his own, he'd thought the photo a good one. But there was no way a photograph could effectively capture the special sparkle of her beautiful eyes, the warmth of her generous smile or the impish dancing of the beauty mark just above her luscious lips.

He frowned, staring at the photo. The beauty mark. In the picture it was on the right side of her lips. But that wasn't right. Omar had kissed that beauty mark a dozen times in the past two weeks—and it was on the left side of her lips.

Unless she'd had plastic surgery to move a beauty mark from one side of her face to the other, which seemed highly preposterous, the woman who had married him was not Elizabeth Fiona Carson.

He picked up the phone on his desk and quickly punched in the numbers that would connect him to his aide. "Rashad, I'm in the main office. Bring me my marriage certificate."

Haley Mercado stood in Harvey Small's office talking to her FBI contact on the phone. "Gotta go," she exclaimed hurriedly when she heard the sound of footsteps just outside the office. She had just hung up the receiver when Harvey came in.

"What are you doing in here?" he asked, his eyes narrowed. "It seems like lately every time I come in, you're here and on my phone."

Haley drew a deep breath to steady her nerves. She placed her hands on her hips in her best imitation of her alter ego, Daisy. "Maybe if I wasn't working so many hours for you, I'd be able to conduct my social life on my own time."

The last thing she needed was to draw any attention to herself, from Harvey or anyone else. If her cover was blown, her life wouldn't be worth a plugged nickel, but it wasn't just her own life she worried about. Pain pressed against her chest, and she consciously tried to will it away.

"I don't give a damn if I'm interfering with your social life. You can consider this office off-limits from now on."

"No problem," Haley said with a forced flippancy as she left the office. It was a problem, but not an insurmountable one. Although for the past several months she'd been using the phone to talk to her FBI contact, she knew the FBI would simply figure out another way.

Still, the moment she was out of Harvey's sight, tears welled in her eyes.

The stress of the past couple of months suddenly seemed too much to bear, and she couldn't control the tears that spilled down her cheeks. All of a sudden her heart was overflowing with all the losses of her life.

The death of her mother and the estrangement from her family were aches deep inside her, but it was the memory of a single night of passion with the man she'd always cared about, and the result of that night, that caused so many tears to fall.

She raced for the employee lounge, needing to get herself under control before starting work. She was grateful to find herself alone, and sank into a chair at one of the tables, fighting for control.

But control was just out of her reach, and she realized the tears that were impossible to stanch had been building inside her for a very long time.

She fumbled in her purse for a tissue as sobs racked her. Her arms ached with emptiness and her heart felt as if it were breaking in two. The tears came faster and faster.

"Hey, girl," Ginger said as she came into the break room. "How's it going?" She stopped and looked at Haley, then sat at the table across from her and grabbed one of her hands. "Daisy? What's wrong?"

Haley couldn't speak. Ginger's fingers tightened around hers, and her youthful face shone with the concern of a good friend.

Haley drew a deep breath as her sobs began to subside. The need to talk about at least a part of her pain was intense, and she knew if she could trust anyone, she could trust this young woman.

"Ginger, if I tell you something, you have to promise me you won't repeat it to anyone."

Ginger's light blue eyes didn't waver from Haley's. "You know you can trust me, Daisy," she replied.

Haley closed her eyes, remembering the sweet scent of baby powder, the snuggly warmth that had once filled her arms—a scent, a warmth now gone.

She opened her eyes, needing to share some of the pain, needing to talk about the heartache that had been a part of her for too long. "You know the baby girl who was found on the golf course six months ago?"

Ginger frowned in confusion. "Sure. Everyone was talking about it when it happened. The last I heard, they still hadn't found out who the mother is."

"I am," Haley said softly, and again the pain came over her in waves. "Her name is Lena and I'm her mother."

She saw the shock that darkened Ginger's eyes, felt it through the fingers that clutched hers.

"What?"

Haley pulled her hand from Ginger's and wiped her cheeks. "She's mine. I arranged for her to be left on the golf course."

She thought of that day so long ago when she'd arranged with Carl Bridges, a judge and her trusted friend, to take baby Lena while she worked undercover. At the time the FBI had arranged for her to work with them, she'd been tormented with fear for her child, and placing her on the golf course where her father was to be playing golf seemed a good plan.

Unfortunately, Lena's daddy hadn't played golf that day. In fact, nobody seemed to know where Luke Callaghan was. So, baby Lena had wound up with Flynt Carson.

"But why?" Ginger asked incredulously. "Why would you leave your baby on the golf course?"

More than anything, Haley wanted to tell Ginger everything, about her real identity and how she was working undercover and helping the FBI by decoding cryptic conversations. But she knew these were things she couldn't tell Ginger. They might put Ginger in danger.

So, instead, in halting words interspersed with tears, she spoke about the ache of not having her baby with her, the ache of knowing everything that she was missing in Lena's life with each day that passed.

"I gave her up for her own safety," she finished by saying.

Once again Ginger reached for her hand and squeezed it tight. "Daisy, what's going on? What kind of trouble are you in?"

Haley shook her head. "I can't tell you anything more, Ginger. I know it sounds overly dramatic and you have no reason in the world to believe me, but if I tell you anything more it might put you in danger."

"Of course, I believe you," Ginger replied. "And I know this, Daisy—I know the kind of loving person you are, and I know only the threat of harm could make you give up your baby girl."

They were words Haley wanted, desperately needed to hear, an affirmation that she'd done the right thing in securing Lena's safety.

"Daisy, is there anything I can do? Any way I can help you?" Ginger asked.

"Pray," Haley said softly. "Pray that I'll be with my baby soon."

# Chapter 11

It had been a magical night, Cara thought as she got into bed to await her husband. She'd felt like a princess in a fairy tale, and Omar had been her knight in shining armor.

The food had been delicious, the band had played everything from traditional Gaspar music to Latin rumbas and good old rock and roll. Yes, it had been a magical night, but she knew the real magic was yet to come.

Two weeks. For two glorious weeks she had been his wife and every day had been like a fantasy. Although his days had been busy with the business of running his country, the early mornings and the evenings had belonged to her.

They had spoken of their future, making plans, teasing about the children they would have and how they would raise them. They'd watched movies together while cuddling together on the big, overstuffed sofa.

Now she stretched languidly across the sheets, thinking of the night to come, a night that promised more of Omar's passion.

A shiver of delight raced up her spine as she remembered the way his dark eyes had caressed her throughout the evening. He'd touched her often, as well, during the celebration, a hand on her back, caressing her arm, stroking her cheek, as if he'd been unable to help himself, and she'd reveled in each of them.

Her heart thudded in anticipation as she heard the door to the bedroom open, then close. A small lamp cast a golden glow to the room, and through the gauzy curtains surrounding the bed, she could see him approach.

He tore the curtains aside, and she sat up as she saw the expression on his handsome features. These were not the features of her loving, gentle husband; rather, his was the countenance of a desert warrior.

"Get up," he commanded, his voice harsh, his eyes glittering with a daunting darkness.

"Why? What's wrong?" She sat up, but he moved away from the bed, allowing the curtain to fall back into place.

Hurriedly she got out of bed and pulled on her robe, her eyes on him. He stood at the doors that led out to the garden, his back to her.

She approached where he stood and placed a hand

on his back. "Omar?" He stiffened at her touch and when he whirled around to face her again, she instinctively took a step backward.

At some point from the time she'd left him, he'd removed the turban he'd worn to the celebration. His black hair was mussed, which usually gave him a charmingly boyish look, but there was nothing boyish about him now.

Not only were his eyes angry, but his entire body seemed to seethe with the emotion. His mouth was a tight slash of suppressed rage.

"You ask me what's wrong? Why don't you tell *me* what's wrong, Cara?" He spat her name as if it were a filthy curse.

The blood seemed to leave her body, replaced by an icy chill, as she realized he knew the truth. Oh God, this wasn't the way it was supposed to happen, she thought frantically. She had wanted to pick the time, the place so she could make him understand. She drew a deep breath, fighting for composure.

"Omar, I wanted to tell you…I tried to tell you…" She reached out a hand toward him again, needing to connect with him, to get past the blackness, the near soullessness of his gaze.

He stepped away from her touch, as if finding the very idea of her hand on him repugnant. "You have made a fool of me, dishonored me and my position." He spat the words angrily. "You have made a mockery not only of me, but of the institution of marriage. Everything we have shared has been based on a lie."

"That's not true," she protested, fighting the tears that threatened. She'd desperately hoped she'd be the one to tell him the truth, that she could explain it all to him rationally and make it all be okay. "Everything we've shared has been based on love."

"Love?" He laughed bitterly. "Don't flatter yourself, Cara. I don't love liars and you are a liar, a woman without honor."

Each of his words was like a bullet shot into her heart, evoking tears of pain and regret. "Omar, I know I should have told you the truth before we married. And every day since our wedding, I've wanted to tell you the truth, but I was afraid."

She could tell by the implacable expression on his face that there was nothing she could say to alleviate his anger. He was immersed in it, wearing it like an impenetrable mantle around him.

She quickly swiped at the tears that had escaped her eyes. "I'm sorry, Omar. Please forgive me. I know what I did was wrong, but I wanted to be your wife, I wanted to share your life."

"You and your sister played a game with my honor, with my future. Perhaps you found the entire thing amusing, a childish game played by twins, but I find nothing amusing about it."

"No, it wasn't like that," she exclaimed.

He drew a deep breath, a forceful arrogance on his face.

"It doesn't matter now. It's done, finished. I've seen the marriage certificate and you are legally my wife."

His gaze was cold and distant. "But don't worry, Cara, I will not divorce you." His voice was laced with disgust. "You will continue to get your wish of being my wife. In public you will continue to be my loving, supportive wife. We will stand united before the people of Gaspar."

Cara sighed with a touch of relief. Maybe it was going to be all right, after all, she told herself. He was angry now, but at least he wasn't demanding that she pack her bags and return to Mission Creek.

"And now you may choose whichever guest room you wish to call your own," he continued. "I will let you know when I wish for you to join me here, but unless you are invited, you are not welcome."

She stared at him in horror. He was banishing her, banishing her from his bedroom, from any piece of his heart where she might have resided. "Omar, please. Don't do this. Let's talk about this."

There was no succor in the dark coldness of his eyes as he gazed at her. "You wanted to be married to me and so we are married. But the conditions of our marriage have now changed. You have changed everything with your lie and manipulation. Now go to bed, Cara. I'll have the servants move your personal belongings from this room in the morning."

He turned away from her, as if he could no longer abide to look at her, and her heart crumbled with despair. She wanted to plead with him, try to make him understand the forces that had driven her to do what she had done.

Did it not count for anything that she had pretended to be her sister because she had fallen in love with him?

Still, she knew now was not the time to try to explain to him. He was beyond angry, and until some of his anger left him, she knew that anything she said would fall on deaf ears.

Surely by morning, after sleeping a night alone, he would soften. Surely by morning he would forgive her and they could continue to build a life together, a life based on love.

With tears still blurring her vision, she walked to the bedroom door, then turned back to look at him.

Once again he stood at the door leading to the garden, only his broad back visible to her. "Omar, I know what I did was wrong, but I was afraid to tell you the truth. I was afraid I would lose you."

He turned, his face a harsh mask of expressionless granite. "Then, your fear has come true, for you have lost my respect and admiration." He presented his back to her again.

The fear Cara had faced when Donny Albright pulled out a gun and pointed it at her was the same kind of fear she felt now. It was the fear of her life.

Staring at Omar's broad back, she saw the shattering of the future she'd hoped to build with him, the destruction of dreams she'd wanted to share with him. The fear of losing him ripped through her, and she ran from the room, from him, stifling the sobs that begged to be released.

She didn't choose one of the spare rooms, she simply ran into the guest room closest to the master suite. It was a spacious room decorated in turquoise and peach. The adjoining full bath was luxurious, but she hardly noticed as she grabbed a washcloth from the closet and buried her face in the soft cotton.

She had known he would be upset when he learned the truth, but she hadn't expected his cold disdain, his unequivocal dismissal of her.

How she wished she could go back in time, back to the moment when he'd first appeared on her doorstep. That had been the time for her full confession, when she should have told him that it was she, and not Fiona, who had been writing to him, she, and not Fiona, who had fallen in love with the beautiful words and the man who had put them together.

But there was no going back now.

She didn't know how long she sat in the bathroom, the washcloth pressed against her face to catch the seemingly endless stream of tears.

Finally, when she was exhausted both mentally and physically, she went back into the bedroom and pulled the spread from the bed, then crawled beneath the cool, crisp sheet.

No scent of Omar lingered in the bed, no welcoming warmth radiated from his body, and her heart ached with the coldness and unfamiliarity of the half-empty bed.

Surely by morning his heart would soften, she told herself. Despite what everyone had told her about sheiks not loving, Cara knew in her heart that Omar loved her. She felt it in his gaze, in his kiss and in his lovemaking. She'd felt it when they spoke of the future, the children they would have and the life they would live.

Or was it simply a crazy hope that made her believe Omar loved her?

She fell asleep with no answer in her heart, only the deep pain of regret and remorse echoing inside her.

No familiar birdsong awakened her, no sweetly drowsy strong male arms pulled her close to herald the new day. She had never felt so alone as she did in that first moment of awakeness the next morning.

The events of the night replayed in her mind, and the tears she'd thought spent threatened to erupt again. But she didn't have time for tears. She had a marriage to save.

It was just after six-thirty when she stepped out of the shower and quickly dressed. Omar usually had his morning coffee between six-thirty and seven, and she wanted to be there with him to see if perhaps some of his anger from last night had subsided.

She hurried toward the breakfast nook, her heart thudding madly in her chest as she saw he was already seated there.

Always before, these early-morning moments had been used as a time for them to connect with each other, to talk about their plans for the day.

But it was evident by the newspaper opened before

him that this morning was going to be different. "Good morning," she murmured, testing the waters.

"Good morning," he replied. His voice was cool, and he didn't look up from the paper.

She poured herself a cup of coffee from the silver carafe on the table, frowning as her gaze lingered on his handsome features. She sipped her coffee, aware of thick tension in the air, a tension she was desperate to break.

"Omar, could we talk?" she finally asked.

His eyes, so dark, so cold, left the paper and glared at her. "We have nothing to talk about. I said everything I had to say to you last night."

"I'm not sure what role you expect me to play in your life."

A smile curved his lips. It was not a pleasant smile. "Your role is to be my good and dutiful wife, to see to my needs and my pleasures."

"And what do I get in return for being a good and dutiful wife?" she asked.

"The admiration of my people and the riches that are mine."

"I don't care about admiration or wealth," she scoffed fervently. She placed her hand on his arm, needing physical contact after a night of isolation and despair.

In the instant that her fingers made contact with his bare arm, she saw a flare of something in his eyes, a spark of warmth. There for a moment, then gone as he moved his arm from her touch and stood.

"I have directed two of the maids to remove your things from the master bedroom. I have a day of meetings and won't be back here until after seven." He didn't wait for her reply, but turned and left the breakfast nook, taking more than a piece of her heart with him.

Omar had never experienced the depth of anger that raged through him, but it was an anger tempered with painful disappointment.

It had taken him hours to fall asleep the night before. He'd tossed and turned, going over every moment of every day he had spent with her, wondering which twin had been with him at which time. Who had written the letters that had so enchanted him?

Over the past three weeks, he'd quoted back to her words she had written to him…but had she been the woman who had written those words, or had her sister?

He'd finally told himself it didn't matter who had done what—the bottom line was he'd been hoodwinked into marrying a woman he hadn't intended to marry.

The marriage was legal and had been consummated, and under no circumstances would he consider a divorce. A divorce would be an admission of a mistake and would undermine his standing with the people of Gaspar.

For better or worse, he was married to Elizabeth

Cara Carson, a woman he didn't even remember meeting at the cotillion so long ago.

The moment he stepped out of his private quarters, Rashad was waiting for him. The little man greeted him with a subdued nod, and instantly Omar realized that Rashad knew what was going on.

"Did you know the truth?" he asked as they walked down the grand stairway.

"Yes," Rashad replied, not even pretending not to know what Omar was talking about.

"How long have you known the truth?"

"Since the day of the marriage," Rashad replied.

A sense of outrage gripped Omar. "And you didn't tell me?"

"I didn't feel it was my place. You seemed happy."

Omar wanted to yell at the man who had been as much a friend as a personal aide, but he bit back the terse words.

"I am very angry, Rashad," he finally said.

"Yes, Your Highness." They walked for a few minutes. Rashad finally broke the silence. "Will you be very angry for long?"

Omar frowned. He felt as if the foundation of all he'd known had disappeared, as if a mask had been ripped off the woman he'd married and beneath the mask was a stranger, a lying, conniving stranger.

"Yes, Rashad," he finally replied. "I think I'm going to be very angry for a long time."

## Chapter 12

It was just after seven that evening when Cara heard Omar enter their quarters. She had spent the day thinking, trying to figure out how to fix what she had broken, how to assuage Omar's anger with her.

If she hadn't seen that flicker of emotion at the table that morning when she'd touched him, she would have spent the day in total despair. But that brief whisper in his eyes had given her an unexpected jolt of hope.

She had dressed carefully for the evening, choosing a long, casual moss-green dress that she knew complemented her eyes and clung to her figure. The neckline was just low enough to give a glimpse of cleavage. She'd put it on with seduction in mind.

She couldn't believe that Omar's desire for her had

died with his knowledge of the truth, and she couldn't believe that his desire wasn't based on loving her. She just had to remind him of those things.

She met him in the living room. "Welcome home, Your Highness," she said demurely. "I took the liberty of drawing you a hot bath to relax you before the evening meal."

He looked at her in surprise. "Why would you do that?"

She gazed down at the floor at his feet. "I'm just trying to be a good and dutiful wife and anticipate your every need."

She held her breath, wondering if she would only manage to stir his ire further with what she'd planned. Surely he would see how sorry she was, how much she loved him, if she played the role he requested of her.

"Fine, a bath sounds good." He didn't look at her again, but instead disappeared into the master suite.

She released the breath she'd held, wishing she'd seen a softening in him, a spark of caring in his eyes, a hint of yearning. But there had been nothing there except the cold darkness that had first appeared the night before.

She waited several minutes, then went into the bathroom. He was already in the tub, and the room smelled of the scented oils she'd added to the hot water.

"What do you want?" he asked, his voice curt.

"The question should be what do you want," she countered smoothly. She grabbed a washcloth from the closet and approached the edge of the sunken tub. "Perhaps my husband would like me to wash his back?"

He didn't reply verbally, but leaned forward and presented her his broad, beautiful back. It was ridiculous how nervous she felt as she bent down at the edge of the tub and wet the washcloth.

She'd stroked his back many times in the course of the past couple of weeks, but this suddenly felt as if it would be her first time touching his smoothly muscled form.

The ache that had been in her chest since the night before intensified as she ran the washcloth across his shoulders.

He was tense, his muscles knotted beneath the skin, and she smoothed the cloth across those muscles in an attempt to relax them. He released a deep sigh, as if finding her actions intensely pleasurable.

What she wanted to do was press her lips against his wet flesh. What she wanted to do was strip off her clothes and join him in the huge tub, see his eyes light with the fires she'd come to love, feel his arms wrap around her.

But she did neither of those things. She was afraid of his reaction, terrified that she'd be rebuffed and her heart would not survive the wound.

As she continued to wash his beautiful skin, she slowed the movement of the cloth across his back, caressing more than washing. He sighed again, a sigh that spoke of exquisite pleasure. It emboldened her, and she moved the cloth lower. She gasped in surprise as he twisted around and grabbed the cloth from her hand.

"That's enough. Thank you, but I'd like to finish my bath alone."

He was aroused. She could tell by his breathing and could see the physical evidence through the clear water as he straightened. A sharp wave of arousal swept her.

It was the desire not just to make love with him, but to have him hold her close enough that she could feel the reassuring beat of his heart, to have him smile at her with sweet gentleness in his eyes.

It was the desire to have everything go back to the way it had been between them, when there had been nothing but sharing and laughter and love.

"Are you sure there's nothing more I can do for you?" she asked softly.

"Your presence is no longer required, Eliza— Cara."

His dismissal hurt, and as she turned and left the bathroom, the pressure of tears ached in her eyes. She told herself she was expecting too much, too soon.

Less than twenty-four hours ago he had somehow learned the truth about her identity. Surely as more time passed, his anger with her would fade and he would realize the woman he'd fallen in love with, the woman he'd wanted to marry, had been she all along.

But the next three days brought no softening of

Omar. They began each day with a silent breakfast.
He read the paper and seemed to ignore her presence.

When they attended a meeting or dinner engagement as a couple, he treated her respectfully but with a
painful distance. And at night, he retired to the master
suite alone; she slept in the bed in the guest room,
wondering if this would be her future with her husband, a future of isolation and loneliness, a future
devoid of love.

When they spent time together alone, she continued
to play the role of devoted wife, drawing his baths,
making certain his favorite foods were served and
doing whatever else she could to please him. She mas-
saged his feet, turned down his bed and tried to anticipate whatever his pleasure might be. She considered
it penance for her sin.

But nothing she did seemed to penetrate through
the shell of indifference he wore around himself. In
the time since they married, she'd discovered Omar
to be a man of enormous sexual appetites and they
had made love every night from the day of their marriage until he'd discovered the truth. It worried her
that four nights had passed and he hadn't touched her
in any way. It worried her that he seemed to have no
problem with not making love to her.

It was early Wednesday morning when she left her
quarters and walked to the other side of the palace
to talk with Hayfa. She needed the advice of another
woman, the advice of somebody who knew Omar well.

Her knock on the door to Sheik Abdul's quarters

was answered by a maid whose physical appearance led Cara to believe the woman was not a native of Gaspar. She was a pretty little woman, about fifty years old, with light brown hair and eyes the color of a cloudless sky.

"I'm here to see Hayfa," Cara said to the woman.

"Of course. If you'll follow me."

"Wait." Cara smiled at the woman. "Your name wouldn't happen to be Jane, would it?"

"Yes, it is." The woman's pale blue eyes widened in obvious surprise.

"And you're originally from Montana?"

She frowned. "How did you know?"

Cara offered her a reassuring smile. "Rashad mentioned you to me."

At the mention of Rashad's name, Jane's cheeks colored slightly. "I can't imagine why that man would bore you by talking about me." Despite her words, Cara could tell that the woman was pleased that Rashad had spoken of her.

"He's very fond of you," she told Jane. "I think with a little encouragement he'd be even more fond of you."

Jane looked at her in surprise, and in her eyes Cara saw the seeds of a romance taking root. That only made her own heartache more intense.

"Hayfa, Jahara and Malika are all in the garden," Jane said as she led Cara through the living area and toward a set of glass doors.

"You don't need to announce me," Cara said, as Jane opened the doors. "I'll find them myself."

The garden was small, but beautifully designed around a marble birdbath fountain. The three women sat at a patio table nearby, their cheerful chatter filling the midmorning air.

"Elizabeth," Malika exclaimed in obvious delight at the sight of her. Hayfa and Jahara greeted her with smiles, as well.

"How nice that you've come to visit," Hayfa said. "We were just about to have some refreshments. Will you join us?"

"Yes, thanks." Cara slid into the fourth chair at the table, wondering how on earth she would broach the subject that was on her mind.

She waited until they had been served refreshing fruit drinks and pastries and had indulged in friendly small talk, then drew a deep breath and began to discuss why she had come to them.

She told them everything from the very beginning. She told them how Fiona had tired of writing to Omar and she had taken over, signing the letters in her sister's name.

She told them of her deception when Omar arrived at her cottage, that she'd intended only to spend a little time with him and then end things.

Finally she told them how her love for Omar and the quickness of their wedding had stymied her attempts to tell him the truth.

"So, how did he find out the truth?" Hayfa asked, her dark eyes giving away nothing of her inner thoughts.

"I don't know," Cara replied miserably. "I only know that since he found out, he's so angry and he doesn't seem to be moving past it."

"Omar is a very proud man," Hayfa replied. "I imagine he feels as if you made a fool of him, tricked him into something he had not intended." She took a sip of her drink. "However, I must confess that I am pleased to learn that you are not Fiona Carson. Your sister appears to be considerably more…spirited than you."

Despite her misery, Cara smiled. "She is, but she's also a loving, wonderful person."

"And your loyalty to her is quite commendable," Hayfa replied. "But you aren't here to discuss your sister's attributes."

Cara nodded. "No, I'm not. I've come to the three of you for some advice." She paused, trying to gather her thoughts. "For the past four days I've done nothing but try to please Omar. I've tried to be the perfect wife, but he isn't sharing any of himself with me."

She looked down at the tabletop. "He's not even sleeping with me," she confessed in a soft whisper.

"Oh, that's definitely not good," Jahara exclaimed. "Physical desire is like the glue that holds together a relationship."

"That's certainly not all there is to a relationship," Hayfa exclaimed. "There are also things like mutual respect and common interests and friendship."

"All very important," Malika agreed, then smiled.

"But, desire is equally important, especially in the beginning of a relationship."

"But I seem to have lost it all—his respect and friendship and desire," Cara said painfully.

"The first and the easiest to get back is the desire." Jahara leaned forward and touched Cara's hand. "I will teach you to dance for Omar."

"Dance for him?"

"A belly dance." She stood, her pretty features radiating girlish excitement. "Come with me to my room and I will teach you a dance of seduction that will surely rekindle Omar's desire."

"Oh, I don't know if that's such a good idea," Cara protested.

"I told you once before that a sheik loves differently than other men," Hayfa said. "That he loves with his head, not his heart. But all men are slaves to desire, and I saw the way Omar looked at you before he found out the truth. His desire for you was great, and getting that back may be the first step in returning your relationship to a good one."

"All right." Cara relented. She wouldn't be satisfied until she'd tried everything in her power to get Omar to forgive her.

If nothing else, the afternoon was good for a few laughs as the three women attempted to teach Cara the fine art of belly dancing.

Cara had always believed herself to be relatively graceful, but time and time again her three mothers-in-law dissolved in giggles as she tried to emulate Jahara's sensual hip and belly movements.

With nothing more pressing on her schedule for the day, she remained with the women until late afternoon, practicing over and over again the movements that looked so simple and sexy, but were difficult to achieve.

When it was time for her to return to her own quarters, the three women made her promise to return the next day for another lesson. She agreed, but her heart wasn't in it. She didn't want to seduce Omar into making love to her. She wanted to seduce him into loving her again.

But that night as she lay in her lonely bed she wondered if anything she could do would make them return to what they'd shared in the first two weeks of their marriage.

What would Fiona do in these circumstances? she asked herself. She had a feeling Fiona would cut her losses and run. She wouldn't stay where she felt unwanted, would never settle for the kind of marriage Cara's had become.

A little over a month ago Cara might have done the same thing. She would have run, run in shame and despair, run with the feeling that she'd never deserved the happiness she'd glimpsed.

But somewhere in the course of the past month she'd become a different woman. She no longer wanted to be like her sister, and she wasn't content being Cara. She had become Elizabeth Al Abdar and that's who she wanted to be, and she intended to fight for her marriage using any tool in her possession. If that meant playing a harem girl and seducing Omar, then, so be it.

Friday afternoon she sat in the living room alone. She'd spent the morning with Hayfa, Jahara and Malika, practicing the dance she hoped would win back Omar.

There was a knock at the door and she jumped up to answer. She'd given the maids the night off, wanting time completely alone with Omar. She didn't know if she wanted to dance for him or yell at him. There was a curious blend of despair and anger growing inside her.

She opened the door to see Rashad standing there, and she greeted him warmly. She hadn't really seen him since the night of the celebration dance.

"Come in," she exclaimed, grateful to see his friendly smile.

He held out a large dress box. "I am to deliver this to you. It is from your esteemed mothers-in-law."

She took the box from him, her curiosity aroused, but kept her attention focused on Rashad. "Can you sit for a few minutes and visit?"

He looked at his watch, then nodded. "Sheik Omar is in a private meeting and it isn't due to break up for a little while. I can sit for a minute or two." He joined her on the sofa.

"How have you been? I've hardly seen you all week," Cara said.

"I've been well." His eyes shone brightly. "And I have a dinner date this evening."

"With Jane?" Cara clapped her hands together in glee as he nodded. "Rashad, I'm so glad."

"I think I have you to thank."

"Trust me, I did nothing more than plant a little seed about you in her head," Cara replied.

"And how are you, Elizabeth?" His eyes gazed at her with a gentleness that told her he knew how difficult things had been.

"So you know the truth," she replied.

"I have known since the day of your wedding."

She eyed him in surprise, then sighed. "Then, you probably also know that Omar is very angry with me."

"Sheik Omar can be a stubborn man."

"I've been told that sheiks don't love like regular men, but I swear, Rashad, if I didn't think Omar loved me, I wouldn't still be here."

"Who told you that sheiks don't love like regular men?" he asked.

"Hayfa…and Omar himself."

Rashad frowned. "I believe that Sheik Abdul married his three wives so his affections would always be divided. It was a protection he created for himself so he would never, ever love as deeply and profoundly as he loved Omar's mother. He did love her deeply, and her loss scarred him. I think he raised Omar to believe that love was not desirable, that to love made a man vulnerable. I think perhaps he was trying to protect his son from the kind of near-mortal wound love had delivered to him."

"But I know Omar is capable of loving."

Rashad smiled. "I told you once that I sense great strength in you. It may take all your strength to overcome Omar's stubbornness and the anger he harbors right now."

He stood. "And now I must go."

Cara walked him to the door, where he turned and smiled at her again, the mischievous grin she loved to see.

"If I were a betting man, Elizabeth Cara Al Abdar, my money would be on you." With these words, he left.

Cara closed the door behind him and went back to the sofa, where the large dress box awaited her. What on earth had the ladies sent over to her?

She pulled the lid off the box and gasped in surprise. Belly-dancing costumes. There were three—one in gold, one in silver and one a deep, lush purple. Each of the harem pants were made of translucent soft chiffon, and the tops were little more than ornately decorated bras.

Her heart expanded as she thought of the three women who had become not only family, but friends.

She carried the box into her bedroom and placed it on the bed. Picking up the gold costume, her heart thudded with anticipation. Could she really do this? Could she put on this risqué costume and dance for Omar?

## Chapter 13

Omar was weary as he made his way from the throne room to his quarters. It wasn't just a bone weariness, but a mental exhaustion as well, and he knew much of it came from the exertion of trying to maintain his anger with Elizabeth.

Even thinking of her name shot a renewed burst of irritation through him. Not *Elizabeth*, he reminded himself. Elizabeth Fiona had been the woman he'd thought he married, the woman he'd intended to marry. Cara was the woman who was now his wife.

Cara, a woman who had been a teacher, a woman who had willingly given him her virginity. Cara, a woman who had spoken to him of her desire for children, her desire to build a family. Cara, a woman who suffered nightmares and who since last week had had nobody to hold her when she awakened afraid and crying in the night.

He shoved this thought aside, even more irritated by the disturbing ache it had evoked in his heart. He nodded to the guards on either side of the door and entered the living room.

Instantly his senses were placed on alert, titillated by the sights and smells that greeted him. The lights were dimmed and the glow of candles filled the room. Incense filled the air along with the tinkling music of the East.

Several of the huge throw pillows had been gathered together to create a place of repose in the center of the floor.

He tensed as he threw his briefcase on the sofa. What was going on? And where were the servants—?

All thought fled from his head as Elizabeth appeared in the doorway between the master suite and the living room.

Electricity sizzled through his veins as his gaze perused her from head to toe. Her dark hair was piled high on her head and entwined with gold braiding. Her eyes glowed a bright emerald, and her cheeks were pink, although he didn't know if the color was natural or cosmetic.

He was stunned by her beauty, displayed to perfection by the brevity of the outfit she wore. The ornate gold bra seemed to be specifically designed to draw attention to her creamy breasts, which spilled over the top of the golden cups.

She wore harem pants that rode low on her hips, the see-through chiffon displaying her shapely legs from ankle to hip. The only concession to modesty was an opaque triangle of material placed strategically in the front of the pants.

"Omar, I didn't hear you come in," she said, and moved across the room with a sensuality he'd never seen before. "Welcome home, my husband," she said. "I've drawn your bath, and when you're finished I'll serve you your meal."

"Where are the servants?" he asked, trying to focus on anything but the desire that swept through him as he looked at her.

"I gave them the evening off," she replied. "And now I need to go check on your dinner."

As she left in the direction of the kitchen, Omar went into the bathroom, wondering what she had planned.

If she thought by cooking him a meal and wearing a provocative little outfit she could somehow ease his disappointment and anger with her, she was sadly mistaken.

Still, moments later as he relaxed in the scented hot water of his bath, he thought of how delicious she had looked, and he couldn't help the physical response that soared through him, a physical response he had no intention of following through on.

A man punishing a woman didn't make love to her, he reminded himself. And he certainly wasn't finished punishing Cara for her dishonesty. He was stronger than any desire he might feel for her.

He finished his bath and pulled on a pair of silk pajama bottoms and a robe, then went into the living room and eyed the pillows she'd apparently arranged for him.

He considered sitting on the sofa just to be perverse, but decided to play along with her game and see where the evening headed.

Stretching out amid the pillows, he closed his eyes for a moment, thinking of the past week. He knew he'd been as ill-tempered as a spitting camel with his staff and knew eventually he would have to make amends.

"A glass of wine?"

He opened his eyes to see her standing near him, a fluted glass in one hand and a platter in the other. "Thank you." He took the glass from her, trying to ignore the poker of heat that stabbed through him as their fingertips met.

She sat down next to him, and his head was momentarily filled with the sweet, achingly familiar scent of her. He quickly swallowed some wine, as if it could clear his head.

"I made you some stuffed grape leaves to begin," she said, and picked up one of the savory rolls that had been cut into bite-size pieces. He parted his lips to receive the bite, trying not to notice the body heat that radiated from her nearness.

"Is it good?" she asked. She sat so close to him

that her warm breath fanned his face. "I got the recipe from the chef. He told me it was one of your favorites."

"It is," he said curtly, and when she offered him another piece, he took it from her fingers instead of allowing her to place it in his mouth.

He didn't want to inadvertently taste her finger, didn't want to dwell on the fact that it had been a week since he'd held her in his arms, kissed her sweet lips, made love to her. "Are you not eating?" he asked.

She shook her head, her eyes beautiful but somber. "I ate before you came home so I could be at your service for the evening." She stood. "I'll be back in just a moment with your entrée."

He watched as she left the room. Her hips swayed with a rhythm that struck a chord deep inside him, and suddenly he wondered who was being punished more by his abstinence—him or her.

The entrée was smothered steak with roasted potatoes, and as Omar ate, Cara sat nearby, her green eyes watching him as if to anticipate whatever he might want or need.

What he needed was to take her into the bedroom and release the physical tension that the past week had built inside him. But he refused to be a slave to his desire.

He ate in silence, although he found himself wondering how she spent the time when he wasn't around. Did she spend long hours alone, perhaps sitting in the gardens surrounded by the flowers she so loved?

She wasn't a woman meant to spend time alone. In the month that they had come to know one another, he had learned that she loved to socialize, to share, to laugh. He missed the sound of her laughter.

When he finished eating, she removed his dishes, then returned to his side. "Would you like me to rub your back? Massage your feet?" Her eyes gleamed with a provocative light. "Or would you prefer that I entertain you by dancing for you?"

Dancing for him? The blood in his veins heated. Although he knew he should tell her he didn't want her entertaining him, he found himself nodding. "Yes, dance for me."

She looked self-conscious as she stood and backed away from him. The glow from the many candles that surrounded them cast a lush golden radiance to her skin, making it appear achingly touchable.

However, he didn't want to touch her, he told himself firmly.

And then she began to dance.

Slowly, sensually she moved to the music, her arms gracefully extended outward as her hips moved in a lover's rhythm.

Her upper body moved, as well, and it looked as if she were offering him the slender column of her neck, the delicate curve of her collarbone, the voluptuous rounded tops of her breasts. He could see the muscles in her shapely legs working, and imagined those legs wrapped around his hips.

A ball of heat flared in the pit of his stomach, suffusing his body as he watched her with narrowed eyes. Who had taught her to move like that? Omar had seen enough belly dancers to know that although her movements were rudimentary and simple, they were the traditional motions of a true belly dancer. He was relatively certain they didn't teach this kind of dancing in Mission Creek, Texas.

Her dainty bare feet brought her closer to him, and again he smelled her fragrance—it dizzied him and made thought next to impossible.

Blood thundered through his veins, and despite his determination to the contrary, desire followed. Her eyes glittered brightly, as if she recognized that she was getting to him.

He didn't *want* to want her, but at the moment he couldn't remember why he'd been denying not only her but himself the pleasure of making love.

He fought to find his anger, but it seemed to have fled him beneath the stronger emotion of desire. As she leaned even closer to him, he stood and grabbed her wrist. She gasped, but stood still, her chest heaving.

"What are you doing, Cara?" he asked softly.

The tip of her tongue smoothed over her lips, and her gaze held his. "I'm dancing for you," she replied, her voice deeper, huskier than usual. "If you will not allow me to share your life as your wife, then perhaps you will allow me to share your bed as a lover would." She punctuated her sentence by opening his robe and leaning into him, allowing her breasts to rub against his chest.

Her words and the contact of her skin against his shattered the last remnant of self-control he'd been desperately clinging to. He grabbed her to him and devoured her mouth with his, reveling in the fullness of her lips, the sweet familiar taste of her.

She welcomed his kiss, opening her mouth to him and wrapping her arms around his neck. He unwound her arms and broke the kiss, then took a step away from her. "Then, you would be happy to be my lover, my harem girl, my love slave?"

"For tonight that would be enough," she replied softly.

She stepped to him, her hips against his, and began to dance again. The friction of her movements against him stirred him in a way nothing ever had before, and he knew she was aware of his intense arousal, knew it by the wicked glitter of her beautiful eyes.

For a torturously long couple of minutes, she brushed her hips against his, then brought her hands up behind her back and released the clasp to her top. She caught the bra before it could fall, holding it against her breasts as her gaze continued to hold his.

"If you wish me to be your love slave, Omar, then, that's what I'll be." She dropped her hands to her sides, allowing the bra to fall to the floor before her.

Omar had never before known that passion could be physically painful, but he ached with it, burned with it, and knew only she could assuage the yearnings of his body.

He sank back to the pillows and pulled her down with him, once again seeking her mouth with his own. At the same time he captured one of her breasts in his hand and could feel her heartbeat thrumming deep beneath the hot, silky skin.

"Elizabeth...Elizabeth," he moaned into her mouth, lost in tidal waves of passion that swept over him, through him. "I have missed the taste of you, the feel of you in my arms."

"And I've missed you," she gasped back, at the same time her hands worked his robe off his shoulders. He removed his arms from the material and allowed it to fall from his body.

He wanted to tell her that this changed nothing, that he was still angry with her, still felt betrayed and manipulated, but he couldn't find the words, not when her mouth moved from his and down his chest.

He moaned as her fingers tugged at the waistband of his silk pajama bottoms, and he lifted his hips to help her remove them.

When he was naked, she stood once again and removed the harem pants that covered her, then rejoined him on the mound of pillows.

He reached for her, but she stopped him. "Just lie back and relax," she murmured. "And let me bring you pleasure."

She moved her hands over his chest, splaying her fingers as if to make as much contact as possible.

Her hands were hot and her eyes held a fevered light as she lightly caressed his upper chest. She smiled at him.

"Your skin feels so good. I love the way it feels."

As her fingers moved to his abdomen, he drew in a sharp breath, surprised to find himself trembling with need.

Her mouth joined her fingers, hotly kissing and nipping at his flesh, moving down his body with deliberate intent. As her mouth and hands moved lower, lower, he tangled his fingers in her hair, fighting for control as pleasure racked his body.

When her fingers wrapped around his hardness, he drew in a sharp breath, knowing if she did anything more it would be over. And he wasn't ready for it to be over.

Cara gasped as he rolled her to her back. He hovered over her, his dark eyes flaming with fires that she knew would consume her. And she wanted to be consumed.

His mouth claimed hers as his hands covered her breasts and his fingers swept over the pebblelike hardness of her nipples.

The contact with her breasts pulled sensations through her entire body, and a sweet familiar tension began to build inside her.

Although the physical aspect of what they were doing nearly overwhelmed her, it was the emotional side of things that brought a shimmer of tears to her eyes.

Surely this would heal the wounds she'd inflicted upon him with her deception. Surely this would make him realize he'd married the right woman, after all, and his anger would finally and forever leave him.

He kissed her with a ferocity that called up a ferocity of her own. She tangled her hands in his hair as their kiss continued.

His hands left her breasts and moved down her sides, across her ribs and to her hips. He gripped her hips as he broke the kiss, and his gaze once again held hers. "If I had to choose a woman I wished to be my love slave, my choice would be you." With these words, one of his hands moved to touch her intimately.

She cried out, unsure which brought her more pleasure, his words or his touch. She only knew that she ached with the need for him, wallowed in the scent of him and was overwhelmed by the feel of his arms around her again.

Closing her eyes, she gave herself to him, as the mastery of his touch swept her higher and higher. As she felt the tension inside her building to an impossible level, she clung to him and shattered.

Immediately he entered her, filling her up with his heat. He moaned deep in the back of his throat, then took possession of her mouth as his hips moved against hers.

She didn't feel as if they were just making love; rather, she felt as if they were rejuvenating the marriage vows they had taken. She felt as if they were reaching across the chasm that had separated them for the past week.

"You are a beguiling love slave," he whispered as his mouth left hers to trail down the length of her neck.

He increased the rhythm of his hips against hers, and she met him thrust for thrust as new need welled up inside her.

She clutched at his back, and whatever control he'd still maintained seemed to break. He groaned, and his movements became frenzied, his strokes shorter and faster.

Wave after wave of pleasure crashed over her. She tried to cry out his name, but the sensations were too intense to allow speech.

He whispered her name as he stiffened against her. She felt him spilling into her, and she hoped they'd make a baby right now, at this moment.

Afterward he rolled to the side of her, his breathing slowly resuming a more normal rhythm. He didn't look at her, but stared up at the ceiling.

A renewed flutter of pain swept through her as she felt his emotional distance. Apparently there was to be none of the afterglow hugging and kissing, whispering and caressing that they'd always enjoyed.

She leaned up on her elbow, gazing at his handsome but stern countenance. How she wished she could place a smile on his features, see his eyes deepen with gentleness, watch his entire face light up with love.

But there was a forbidding harshness to his features that held her at bay. "Is there anything else my husband would like his love slave to do for him?" she asked with a forced lightness in her tone.

He turned his head, his gaze lingering on her for a moment. In the depth of his impossibly dark eyes she tried to find a hint of any positive emotion. But there was nothing warm, nothing tender, nothing yielding there.

"I have no further need of you for the evening," he said as he sat up and grabbed his robe. "It's been a long day and I'm just going to retire to my bed." He stood. "I'll see you in the morning."

As he left the living area and disappeared into the master suite, Cara wondered if he had any idea how his callous dismissal of her cut through her very soul.

She stood, feeling vulnerable and stupidly naked, and quickly grabbed for the pieces of the belly dancing costume. It had certainly achieved its purpose, having seduced Omar into making love to her once again.

But she had wanted so much more. She had wanted their lovemaking to lead to his forgiveness. She'd wanted it to remind him of all she could give him, would give him as his wife.

As she put the pillows back where they belonged, then carried the dishes to the kitchen, she wondered how long she would be cast in the role of love slave?

When would he decide that she had done enough penance?

What if he *never* forgave her? What if he intended to have her play the role of love slave for the rest of their married lives?

Could she do that? Could she let him take his physical pleasure from her and offer her nothing more? Could that ever be enough for her?

*Where's your self-respect?* a voice whispered in the back of her head. She recognized the voice. It wasn't her own, but Fiona's.

Cara knew that her sister would never allow a man to treat her the way Omar had treated Cara for the past week. But Fiona hadn't lied…and Fiona didn't love Omar. Did she, Cara, love Omar enough to continue to be satisfied with only her husband's physical desire for her and nothing more?

"Sir, we just got word that Commander Westin has been taken by the enemy and is being held about twenty-five miles from here." The soldier stood at attention in front of where Luke sat at a desk.

At the news, Luke stood, shocked. "Do we have any other details?" he asked tersely.

The young soldier shook his head. "That's all we know at this time."

"Thank you, that will be all." Luke dismissed the soldier, needing time to digest, time to assess.

He and a band of soldiers had spent weeks in the jungle, fighting terrorists, attempting to gain ground.

After those weeks, exhausted and filthy, they had returned to the military base where they now had been for two days.

Luke eased back into his chair, frowning as he thought of Phillip Westin in the hands of the enemy. Phillip Westin was not just a commander, but a friend, a man who had once saved Luke's life.

It had been during the Gulf War. Luke and four of his buddies—Ricky Mercado, Tyler Murdoch, Flynt Carson and Spence Harrison—had been on a mission, spying on an enemy camp.

Somehow, a round of ammunition had inadvertently gone off in Tyler's gear and the five of them had been captured. They had been held for six weeks. Half-starved and given just enough water to keep them alive, the men had stared their own mortality in the face.

Phillip Westin had orchestrated a daring rescue and had managed to get all of them out of there alive, creating a lasting bond among them.

And now Phillip was in trouble and Luke would do everything in his power for the man he cared about and respected, the man who had once saved his life.

His mind worked to develop a plan of attack, and the first man he thought of to aid him in attempting a rescue of Phillip was Tyler Murdoch.

Luke knew Murdoch had a reputation as a lone wolf, but he was a tough man and a bomb expert, and Luke knew those qualities would come in handy on a job like this. Besides, Murdoch owed Phillip his life, too.

Luke stood, energized with determination. He'd see that Tyler was brought in, he'd find out as much as he could about Westin's exact location and condition; then it was time for action. Time to pay back a debt.

# Chapter 14

Omar fought off irritation and tried to concentrate on the physical pleasure of his wife massaging his back with sensual oil.

For the past two nights, she'd been at his beck and call. Wearing breathtakingly sexy belly-dancing costumes, she'd played the role of harem girl, dancing for him, pleasuring him in a thousand ways and making love to him.

Tonight she had met him at the door wearing a deep purple outfit that had absolutely stunned him. The dark, plush color had brought out the lush creaminess of her skin tones and made her eyes seem impossibly green.

It had been late when he'd come in, long after dinner and just before his usual bedtime. He'd assumed she would already have retired to her room, but she'd greeted him at the door and offered him a back massage.

Most men would revel in his position. He was a powerful, wealthy sheik in charge of a prosperous, peaceful country. His wife was a credit to him in all public appearances and a superb lover in privacy.

However, Omar wasn't satisfied. In fact, with each passing day he grew more dissatisfied—and he knew the reason. While he had certainly been drawn to Cara's physical attractiveness and sensual nature, he'd also enjoyed her intelligence, her quick wit and her laughter during the weeks that he hadn't known the truth about her identity.

And those were all of the things his anger had deprived him of. The problem was, he still wanted to hang on to his anger toward her. The lie she had perpetrated on him was immense, and he refused to find forgiveness in his heart.

Still, anger was difficult to maintain beneath the gentle massage of her warm hands and with her perfume wafting in the air.

She straddled his back on the large master bed, and each time she worked her hands up to his shoulders, her upper body made warm contact with his.

He wanted her again. Despite the fact that they'd made love last night and the night before, he wanted her again with an intensity that surprised him.

"That's enough," he said. "If you relax me any more I shall be asleep, and I'm not ready to sleep yet."

She scooted off him and left the bed, and he turned over on his back and looked at her. The purple harem outfit transformed her from beautiful into stunning. It displayed her physical attributes to perfection.

But when had her eyes lost their brilliant sparkle? When had her features become so drawn, so utterly lifeless? For just a moment, a brief moment, sadness flooded him as he looked at her unsmiling countenance.

"I'm glad you aren't ready to sleep yet, Omar, because we need to talk."

Instantly his defenses kicked in. He sat up and eyed her through narrowed eyes. "I can't think of anything we would need to talk about."

She held his gaze steadily. "We need to talk about us."

He frowned and got out of the bed, summoning the anger that was never far from the surface. He pulled on his robe, then looked at her again. "There's nothing to discuss," he said.

Her chin lifted, and for the first time that evening sparks appeared in her eyes. "Perhaps you have nothing to say on the subject, but I have some things to say."

"That doesn't mean I have to listen," he replied, and stalked into the bathroom.

But she refused to allow his escape, and followed him to the shower, where he started the water running in a steamy stream.

"For heaven's sake, Omar, how long do you intend to continue to punish me?"

He didn't answer her, but stripped off his robe and stepped into the shower. He remained beneath the hot water for a long time in an attempt to tamp down the desire that had roared through him minutes earlier, also recognizing that he was using the shower as an escape from a conversation he didn't want to have.

But he had underestimated her determination. When he shut off the water and stepped from the shower confines, she stood in front of him, a towel in hand.

"Please, Omar, just listen to what I have to say." Her eyes held an appeal he found difficult to resist.

"Speak your mind, then be done with it," he exclaimed as he dried off, then pulled on his pajama bottoms. He left the bathroom with her following right behind him.

"Come with me to the breakfast nook. I'll make us some coffee. I'm begging you, Omar. Just a few minutes of your time."

He sighed and raked a hand through his damp hair. "All right," he relented. It was probably better that they talk in the kitchen rather than in the bedroom, which was filled with memories of a happier time.

He followed her to the huge kitchen and sat at the table in the breakfast nook, watching as she moved across the room to the coffeemaker.

If it weren't for the placing of the beauty mark on her face, he never would have known that she wasn't

Elizabeth Fiona. If he hadn't realized the truth himself, would she never have told him? Had she just assumed that he would never learn the truth?

Once again anger roared through him. Had her deception been the result of bored jet-setting sisters plotting a little fun at his expense? He couldn't imagine what had possessed her to play such a game, or how he had been so blinded by her seeming innocence.

By the time she placed a cup of coffee in front of him and joined him across the table, his anger was as rich and bold as it had been the night of the celebration dance when he'd first discovered the truth.

She was nervous. She licked her lower lip twice, her fingers trembling slightly as she reached for her cup. Instead of taking a sip of the hot brew, she wrapped her fingers around the cup, as if needing the warmth to calm her.

"Omar, I have done a terrible thing," she began. "And I'd give anything in this world if I could go back and undo it, but I can't."

She paused, as if waiting for him to say something, anything, but he didn't speak. He took a sip of his coffee and continued to gaze at her.

Her cheeks pinkened and she gazed down at the tabletop for a moment, then looked at him once again, a hint of tears in her beautiful eyes. "I tried to tell you the truth before we got married. But every time I managed to get up my nerve, something else would interfere."

"If you had wanted me to know the truth, you

would have found the time and place to tell me," he responded coolly.

Again her cheeks stained with color. "You're right," she finally said. "But you quoted words from my letters back to me. You made me believe you'd fallen in love with the woman who had written those letters, and I had already fallen in love with you."

So at least one of the questions he'd entertained had been answered. The letters that had touched him had been written by her, not the woman he'd thought to make his bride.

"I told you, Omar, that what I did was terrible," she continued. She stood abruptly and began to pace the floor in front of the table, tears once again gleaming in her eyes. "I had been hidden in the shadow of Fiona for most of my life. You have no idea what it's like to grow up with a twin who is so bright, so beautiful and desirable."

She paused and drew a deep breath, her voice softer as she continued. "I'm not trying to make excuses for what I did, but I do want to try to explain."

"The reasons that drove you are unimportant," he replied, refusing to be moved by anything she might say.

"Perhaps they are unimportant to you, Omar, but they are important to me." She sank back into the chair opposite him. "When you first showed up at my cottage, I was stunned, and I told myself there was no real harm in having just one meal with you. Then I walked into that private dining room that you had filled with flowers, and I realized I was in love with you."

Despite his intention to the contrary, her words slipped through his anger to pierce his heart. He got up from the table, needing to distance himself, needing to break eye contact with her, for in her eyes he saw her heart.

"What I did by keeping the truth from you was wrong, Omar," she exclaimed, the sound of a sob rising in her voice. "But I did it because I loved you and I was so afraid that if you found out the truth, you wouldn't want a pale, sorry imitation of the vivacious, beautiful woman you had seen at that cotillion so long ago."

Omar slammed a fist down on the countertop. "You made a fool of me." The words ripped from his throat. "You made a mockery of our marriage."

Wearily she nodded her head. "So, how long do you intend to punish me, Omar? Weeks? Months? Years? My crime was a lie based on love for you. Please, tell me what my sentence is to be."

"You talk too much about love," he said angrily. "I told you before, a sheik doesn't love the way normal men love."

"Stop saying that. Who told you that, anyway?" For the first time since they'd begun their conversation he saw a flash of anger in her eyes.

She rose and walked over to where he stood, stopping mere inches from him. As always, the scent of her stirred him, which only increased his ire.

"Was it your father?" she asked. "Because if it was, then he lied to you, and I have a feeling if you ask him about your mother, you'll discover that sheiks *do* love." Tears tracked down her cheeks. "And if you don't love me, can't love me, then, please let me go. Divorce me."

He reached out, grabbed her and pulled her tight against him. "Never. I don't give up what is mine. I will never divorce you."

He could feel her heartbeat against his chest, the frantic flutter of a captured bird. Her cheeks were wet with her tears, and he fought the impulse to reach up and gently wipe them away.

"If you won't divorce me, then, forgive me," she said softly.

"I can't do that," he said stiffly.

Like a dervish wind, she spun out of his arms and stepped away from him. Her eyes glistened with the remnants of her tears and a renewed flare of anger. "If you cannot find it in your heart to forgive, then, you will never be a great sheik, only an adequate one. You can't be a good ruler and not have any forgiveness in your soul." Tears once again spilled from her eyes. "And if you can't forgive me, then, you aren't the man I thought you were."

She laughed bitterly. "You thought I was my sister when you married me, and I thought you were a man with a loving heart and a gentle soul. I'd say we're even when it comes to deception." She turned and ran from the kitchen before he could reply.

He returned to the table and sat down, trying to forget the sight of her tearstained face, the depth of emotion in her voice.

He finished drinking his cup of coffee, then shut off the coffeemaker and went to his bed, where her perfume lingered in the air.

Sleep was a long time in coming for Omar that night. Cara's words danced in his head, while the thought of her woeful tears ached in his chest.

Damn her. Damn her for confusing him. A sheik was not supposed to entertain confusion, especially when it came to a woman. And a sheik was supposed to guard his heart when it came to love. Wasn't that what he'd heard over and over from his father?

And what had she meant by telling him to speak to his father about his mother? What could she know of her father's relationship with the woman who had died at his birth?

He awakened the next morning later than usual and left immediately for a morning of meetings. But he found it difficult to concentrate on business.

Cara consumed his thoughts. Her words about him never being a great sheik because of his unforgiving nature rankled.

He wanted to be a great leader for his people. He had a feeling she had said that just to hurt him. It had been another manipulation to try to get her way, to try to get him to forgive her.

But how could he forgive a woman who had lied about something as basic as her name, a woman who had taken his name in a legal ceremony under false pretenses?

When he'd looked at the marriage certificate, he'd realized that at least she hadn't lied on it. She'd signed it Elizabeth C. Carson.

He looked at Rashad, who sat at his right hand and was taking notes. Rashad had known the truth but hadn't told him. Rashad had let his feelings about Cara be known. He adored her, and he'd been unable to hide his displeasure with Omar this past week.

*Elizabeth Cara Carson.* Her name went around and around in his head. *What difference does her middle name make?* a tiny voice asked. *She makes you happy, so what difference does it make if her beauty mark is on a different side of her lips?*

By the time his morning meetings were finished, he was feeling irritable and tired. But he decided to seek out his father, bothered by what Cara had said to him the night before.

He found Sheik Abdul in the garden with his three wives. His face lit with pleasure as Omar approached where they sat at the patio table.

"My son, what a pleasant surprise," Sheik Abdul exclaimed.

Hayfa stood to offer her son her chair. He kissed her on the cheek, then sat in the chair she had vacated. "Have you come for lunch?" Hayfa asked.

"No, thanks. But I would like a few minutes alone with my father."

"Certainly," Hayfa replied, as the other two women rose from their chairs.

Sheik Abdul waited until his wives were out of sight, then he turned to his son, his dark eyes filled with speculation. "I have heard through the grapevine that the past several days my son has had the sting of a scorpion."

Omar frowned. "A bit of an exaggeration," he said defensively. His father continued to gaze at him, his eyes sharp and wise. "All right, I'll admit it, I have been rather irritable lately," he finally confessed.

"The oil negotiations are finished?" Sheik Abdul asked.

Omar nodded. "A fair arrangement that will assure Gaspar future prosperity."

"Then, it isn't business that has you unusually contentious?"

Omar sighed and looked away from his father. Flowers. Everywhere around them were flowers, and of course his thoughts turned to his wife.

Within minutes he was telling his father everything—about the letters he had written and the ones he had received, letters he'd assumed had been from Fiona. He told his father about Cara's lie and how he had only realized the truth the week before, after the celebration dance. He repeated to Sheik Abdul what Cara had told him, about why she'd done it and why she hadn't told him the truth.

"So, what do you intend to do?" his father asked

when he'd finished speaking. "Do you wish to divorce her?"

"No." The answer sprang quickly to his lips. "We are married, and I have no intention of changing that fact."

He frowned and eyed his father steadily. "Tell me about my mother."

Pain darkened his father's eyes. "What does she have to do with any of this?"

"I'm curious, that's all. You never speak of her."

"There is no point in speaking of her. She is gone."

There was a tension in his father's voice, a whisper of pain that surprised Omar. "Father, I have always believed you are a wise man, and it was you who taught me that sheiks don't love with their hearts, that to love is a form of weakness. Did you love my mother?"

Sheik Abdul averted his gaze from Omar's and instead focused on some point in the distance. For a moment silence reigned between the two men. Omar waited patiently, knowing eventually his father would answer his question.

"Antonia was like no other woman I had ever met," he finally said. "She was like the joyous birdsong of a new morning, a cool cloth on a fevered brow. Had I not been a sheik, she'd have made me feel like one. She gave me laughter and joy, friendship and passion."

He looked at Omar again, his eyes radiating the emotion that was in his heart. "Did I love her? Aside from you, I have never loved anyone as profoundly, as deeply as I loved Antonia. When she died, she took with her any capacity I might have had to love another woman in that same way."

So, this must have been what Cara had wanted him to hear, Omar thought. He recognized that his father's admission of loving his mother certainly belied what his father had tried to teach him about love.

"My son." Sheik Abdul reached across the table and gripped Omar's hand firmly in his. "I have done you an enormous injustice in attempting to shield your heart from love. My only excuse is that I never wanted you to feel the kind of pain I felt when I lost your mother."

He released Omar's hand, then leaned back in his chair. "You were so in love with this Fiona?"

"No," Omar scoffed. "I only met her once, years ago. She was quite beautiful, but no more so than Cara. It was the letters I received that captured my heart." *Captured his heart.* His own words surprised him, and suddenly he realized why he was so angry with Cara.

He stood abruptly. "I must go," he said. "I need to discuss some things with my wife."

"Take care, son," Sheik Abdul exclaimed. "A woman's heart is a fragile thing."

Omar nodded. "I know. However, I have suddenly come to realize that in love, all hearts are created equal." With these words, Omar left his father at the table and headed for his quarters—and Cara.

"Elizabeth…Cara," he called the moment he walked into their quarters.

There was no reply. He walked down the hallway to the bedroom that she had been using since he'd banished her from the master suite.

The room was neat, the bed made, and everything in order. He turned to leave the room and nearly ran over one of the maids. "Ah, Sahira, where is my wife?" he asked.

"I don't know, Your Highness. She called for a car about an hour ago and left."

"She didn't mention where she was going?" he asked.

"She did not say…but she had a suitcase with her."

"A suitcase!" Shocked, he raced back into the bedroom and flung open the closet door. Most of the clothing she had brought with her was gone.

"Guards!" he yelled.

## Chapter 15

She would be home in plenty of time to shop for
Christmas.

Cara stared out the glass windows of the Gaspar
public airport, trying not to think of all she was leaving behind: the haunting beauty of Gaspar, the friend-
liness of the people and, most importantly, Omar.

She looked at her watch and frowned. Upon arriving, she had quickly discovered that the small Gaspar
airport had only about twenty flights in and out daily,
none of which was a direct flight to the United States.

With changing planes and layovers, it would be
twenty hours or so before she got back to her little
cottage in Mission Creek, Texas.

She turned away from the window when the landscape blurred from her ever-present tears. She picked

up her suitcase and walked to a row of chairs, sinking down in the last one, nearest the gate where she would eventually board her plane.

Drawing a deep breath, she thought over the events of the night before. Her love for Omar hadn't changed. It burned in her heart, seared through her soul, but she'd realized after her argument with him that she couldn't remain with him.

She refused to play his love slave for another day, another minute. She loved him, but she loved herself too much to be satisfied with just his physical love and nothing more.

Funny, the Cara she had been before meeting him might have stayed, might have been desperate and willing to accept whatever crumbs he was willing to throw in her direction. But in his love she'd found her own strength—the strength to walk away from him and his unforgiving eyes.

Aside from Omar, there were many things she would miss, like the friendships she had made with his stepmothers. Hayfa, Jahara and Malika would always have a special place in her heart, but even their friendship couldn't make her stay another minute.

She would not be subservient to any man—not even Omar, who seemed to feel she owed it to him because of her deception. She had apologized and she had loved him and that should be enough for him, but of course it wasn't.

Again tears stung her eyes, and she closed them, willing the tears away. After leaving Omar in the kitchen the night before, she had cried enough tears to last two lifetimes.

Something good had survived despite the heartache. She no longer had any desire to be just like her sister. In the weeks that she had spent with Omar before he'd realized the truth, she had found herself. Maybe someday she would be able to thank him for that.

She consciously willed her thoughts away from Omar and instead thought of her little cottage and the life she was returning to. Her life would be different there because *she* was different. She wasn't sure what the future held for her, but she would never again feel as if she were functioning in the shadow of her sister.

"Your Highness?" A deep voice spoke from behind her as a hand touched her shoulder.

She turned in her seat to see three uniformed palace guards. "Yes?"

"We are here to accompany you back to the palace," the eldest of the three said.

"Thank you, but that isn't necessary," she replied. "I have no intention of returning to the palace."

The guard frowned, looking pained. "I'm afraid our orders are to take you back to the palace." The other two guards stepped closer.

Cara stood and faced the three of them. "Well, I'm changing your orders," she retorted.

"Your Highness, we take our orders from Sheik Al Abdar, and he has ordered us not to return without you."

Cara watched in horror as one of the guards pulled out a pair of handcuffs. "You have got to be kidding me," she exclaimed. She looked from one very serious face to the other.

"We can do this the easy way, or we can do it the hard way," the guard explained. "It's entirely up to you."

Cara had the wildest impulse to run for the ladies' room, but she had a feeling they would follow her in without a second thought. They were on a mission, doing their sheik's work, and nothing was going to deter them.

"Oh, for heaven's sake," she exclaimed with aggravation. She picked up her suitcase and looked at them expectantly. "Fine, take me back and let's get this over with."

A car awaited them at the curb. She was placed in the back with a guard on either side, and she steeled herself for what was to come.

Apparently Omar wanted a final confrontation. Fine, he would have one. His high-handedness in sending guards for her only confirmed that he was a man without a heart, a man who had fooled her as completely as she had fooled him.

The ride to the palace was a silent one. The guards seemed uncomfortable, and she wondered how many times in the past they'd had to hunt down and bring back one of Omar's women.

Probably never, she thought. She would guess that women didn't leave Omar. Omar left women.

Well, he was about to experience a first. Her mind was made up. She would not stay and play his game of love.

Still, as the palace came into view, tears once again threatened, and her chest tightened with a suffocating ache. This was to have been her home, the place where she would have children and grow old with her husband.

Now the palace represented only the pain of dreams lost, of futures forsaken and love denied. She hoped he didn't intend to make this difficult on her.

It would be nice if her last impression of Omar was one of acquiescence and not one of pride and anger. She just wanted him to let her go.

"We are to escort you directly to the throne room," the guard said as they exited the car.

*The throne room.* So, he was to meet with her in a room where the aura of his power was almighty. He didn't want to meet with her as husband and wife, but as sheik and his property.

A surge of anger displaced her pain, and she wrapped that anger around her like a defensive suit of armor as she stalked toward the throne room.

He sat on the oversize, ornate chair that was his throne. He was in full sheik costume, wearing a long white silk robe with gold embroidery and a white turban trimmed in tiny gold beads. The white made the darkness of his eyes more profound and the hue of his skin richer and deeper.

She could tell even from a distance that he had an

arrogant tilt to his head. His mouth was a harsh slash of displeasure as he eyed her. He looked every inch the powerful ruler, every inch the handsome man she loved.

"You would leave me?" His voice thundered in the otherwise empty, cavernous room.

She hesitated a moment, then replied. "You had already left me." Her voice sounded small, tinny, and she cleared her throat self-consciously. "Did you know your guards were going to handcuff me to get me back here?"

"They had their orders to do whatever necessary to return you to where you belong."

"I don't belong here," she exclaimed, and fought against the thick emotion that tried to crawl up her throat.

"Come closer, dear wife. I want to look into your eyes when I speak with you."

She remained in place. "We have nothing to talk about."

He stood. "I have much to talk about."

"You can talk, but that doesn't mean I'll listen," she replied with a forced coolness in her tone.

Her heart fluttered with nervous tension as he stepped off the dais and approached where she stood. His eyes seemed to glitter like those of an animal, and he moved with an athletic grace.

"You had your say last night. Now it's my turn." He stopped when he stood mere inches from her, his breath warm on her face, his body heat radiating outward as if to banish her coolness.

"You've had your say for the past week," she replied, trying not to dwell on how handsome he looked, how much she wanted to reach out and touch him, throw her arms around him. "You had your say by avoiding me, refusing to share with me, expecting me to attend to your every need while giving me nothing in return."

"Ah, but I seem to remember giving you something," he replied, his voice as deep, as smooth as a caress.

Frustration rose inside her. "I'm not talking about sex, Omar." She took a step back from him, needing some distance. "A month ago perhaps I would have been satisfied with whatever you were willing to give to me. My self-esteem was low, and in my mind I was existing in Fiona's shadow. I just wanted something for my own."

"And you don't want that anymore?" he asked.

"Of course I still want that," she replied. "But I'm no longer the woman I was a month ago. I know I'm worth more than what you've given me this past week."

She raised her chin. "And I'm not willing to settle anymore. I did a bad thing and I've apologized and tried to make it up to you, but you refuse to find any forgiveness in your heart."

Emotion pressed thick and hot against her chest. "I deserve more, Omar. I deserve to be loved."

"And now you will listen to me," he said.

Once again he moved toward her, breaching the distance she'd placed between them. "I have finally realized the root of my anger with you." His gaze bore into hers. "It isn't necessarily that you lied, but that you felt the *need* to lie."

She frowned. "I don't understand."

His nostrils thinned slightly and his eyes narrowed. Power radiated from him, a power and arrogance that was daunting. "My anger comes from the fact that you thought I was so shallow, so superficial, that I would want only the woman I'd met briefly six years before at a dance. My anger comes from the fact that you really believed that despite the letters we exchanged, in spite of the time we spent together, I would choose Fiona over you."

He reached out a hand and stroked a strand of her hair, his eyes less fierce than before. "When I traveled to Texas, I had every intention of marrying Elizabeth Fiona Carson because I believed she was the woman who had written those beautiful letters to me. Then we spent time together, and I fell in love with you. How could you think me so superficial as to negate everything we shared because of a name?"

Cara was confused and found it difficult to think with him lightly caressing her hair. Again she stepped back from him, trying to assess everything he had just said. Had he really said he'd fallen in love with her?

"Omar, I didn't underestimate you. Don't you see? I underestimated myself," she said.

She gasped as he pulled her into his arms. "Then, we must see that you don't make that same mistake in the future," he said.

"I'm going back home, Omar." She struggled half-heartedly to get out of his embrace, but he held tight.

"You are home," he replied.

The sweet timbre of his voice cascaded warmth through her, a warmth she'd been bereft of for the past week. She steeled herself against it, refusing to succumb to his macho charms.

"No, Omar. Home is where dreams are spun and lives are shared. Home is where love resides. Real love, not sexual love." To her intense displeasure, tears trickled from her eyes. She reached up to wipe them away, but he got there first and wiped them away with his thumbs.

"Then, you are truly home right now, Cara," he said softly.

She looked at him and was surprised to see a depth of vulnerability in his eyes.

"When I realized you were gone, I also realized all that I was about to lose," he said, and pulled her even closer against him.

"I've given much thought this morning to the concept of love," he continued. "You were right. I was taught that love made a man weak, that the romantic kind of love women yearned for was fine for regular men, but taboo for a sheik."

Again she tried to wriggle out of his embrace, but

he held fast to her. The vulnerability in his eyes transformed to a shine of desperation.

"Cara, please listen to me. As I waited for my guards to return you to me, I thought of my life without your laughter, my life without your dreams. I thought of my life without you, and there was nothing in my heart but pain. I realized that it didn't matter what my father tried to teach me. I love you, Cara. I love you with all my heart, all my soul. Please, don't leave me."

He'd never looked less like a sheik and more like a man than he did at that moment. His dark eyes shone with an intensity that momentarily stole her breath, as the impact of his words created a dizzying joy inside her.

"I don't want to leave you," she said, her voice trembling with emotion. The words were barely out of her mouth before he crushed his lips to hers, kissing her in a white-hot fever that spoke not just of passion, but of love.

"Stay and build dreams with me," he said when they broke the kiss. "Stay and share my life with me. Share a future of love, and build a family with me."

Her heart was joyous as she felt his love flowing from every pore in his body, filling her up with happiness. "No more love slave?" she asked.

He smiled, that wonderfully teasing smile that had captured her heart on the first day they had met. "Maybe just on our anniversaries," he said. "We'll take turns. You'll be my love slave and I'll be yours."

She smiled up at him. "I think you already owe me a turn."

He gripped her to him, and she laid her head against his broad chest. She could hear his heartbeat, pounding the language of love.

"I am a sheik, Cara. I am wealthy and powerful and greatly esteemed by the people of my country. But I feel as if without you I would have nothing, I would be nobody."

"Omar." She placed a hand on his cheek. "With or without me you would be a wonderful man, but it's nice that you think I'm a necessity."

"My love, you are," he said fiercely. "Now and always." With those words of promise, he captured her lips once again, this time in a gentle, giving kiss that made her very happy that she was not Fiona Carson, but Elizabeth Cara Al Abdar, beloved wife of Sheik Omar Al Abdar.

\* \* \* \* \*